Pumping Up Napoleon

and other Stories

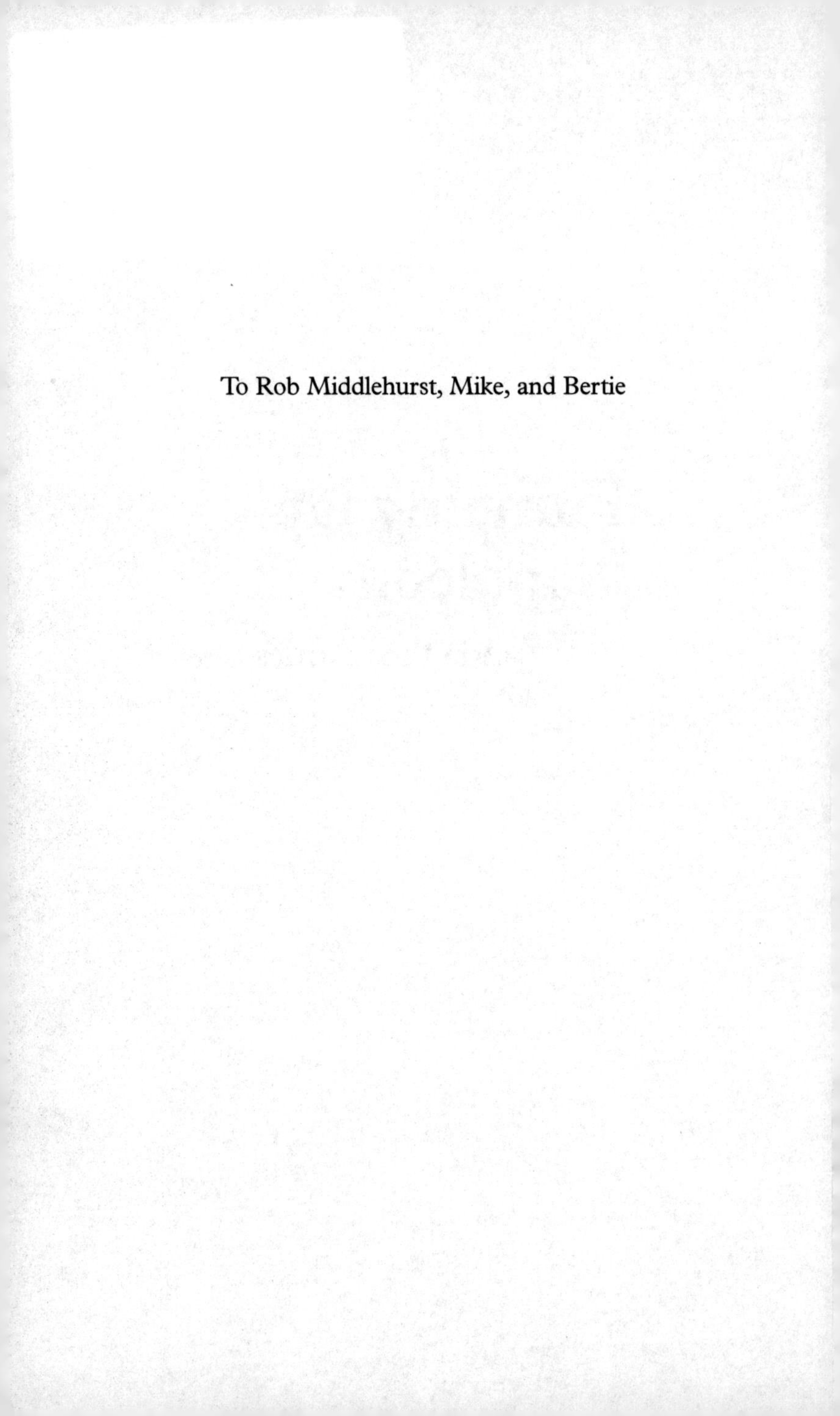

To Rob Middlehurst, Mike, and Bertie

Maria Donovan

Pumping Up Napoleon

and other Stories

seren

Seren is the book imprint of
Poetry Wales Press Ltd
57 Nolton Street, Bridgend, Wales CF31 3AE
www.seren-books.com

ISBN 978-1-85411-441-9

A CIP record for this title is available from the British Library.

Cover design: matt joyce
www.themeekshall.co.uk

The publisher works with the financial assistance of the Welsh Books Council.

Printed in Plantin by CPD (Wales), Blaina

Contents

Pumping Up Napoleon

That summer Napoleon Bonaparte started wearing shorts, which made Marjorie Campbell question her feelings for him. In her opinion only very good legs should risk exposure in an urban setting – and even then… Besides, and disappointingly, of the bare parts of Napoleon she'd seen so far, his legs were the least attractive: a dirty grey colour, mottled with blue; knees like dried porridge.

He sat in her University office with his feet up on the desk, flapping his hands to show that he was hot. Through the autumn, winter and spring, he had appeared in a series of elegant high-collared suits, which Marjorie had admired. He had worn white gloves to disguise the decay of his fingertips, and boots of polished leather. Now he was wearing sandals and his toes were black.

Marjorie had been in love with Napoleon for some time before his resurrection. She was one of those women who have to be in love with someone. It was a kind of addiction, something she aspired to control by only allowing herself to become enamoured of men she couldn't have.

Her admirers had always been mainly fictional. They visited for five minutes at bedtime, inevitably said the right thing and knew exactly when to shut up. The bliss of being able to roll over and fall asleep without thinking of someone else's needs and desires.

Best of all, not having to take an interest in another human being left her plenty of time for her career. Marjorie was a historian, with a special interest in the English Civil War. Napoleon wasn't her first character from history. She'd always had a bit of a thing about Prince Rupert (those lovely brown eyes, that secretive smile) and visited him in the National Portrait Gallery every summer.

On one such occasion she came across two men in overalls carrying a large picture of Napoleon down a long corridor. She recognised him because of the hat. He was standing with his back to her on a cliff looking out across a dark sea. The sky was stormy black save for a bright light on the horizon. What was he looking at? A sunset? Or the coast of England under a new dawn? The Emperor's legs, she noticed, were well shaped, his body compact. She couldn't see his face, but that didn't matter. By the time she left the Gallery that day, Marjorie had forgotten Rupert and fallen in love with the ambition and energy bunched in the muscles of Napoleon's white-breeched behind.

Back at home, she looked him up on the web and found evidence of his passionate nature. So impatient was he to be with his new bride, Marie Louisa (he'd already done and dumped Josephine) that he galloped up to meet her on the road, stopped her carriage and leapt in, all wet with rain, to demand his conjugal rights – before the marriage ceremony had properly taken place. Just right for me, thought Marjorie.

The Emperor of France visited Marjorie on several occasions after that. He had to tear himself away from wars and law-making to be with her, but she was worth it. In her dreams it was always the young and passionate Napoleon who came to her, not the bored, fat Napoleon who tried to grow vegetables on St Helena.

She felt a little guilty about Rupert. But now that it was over, she could admit he had an air of infidelity about him. She'd always suspected he was secretly laughing at her.

Napoleon's real-life resurrection caused Marjorie some consternation. The first she knew of it was when Amnesty International started a letter-writing campaign calling for the release of all persons experimentally brought back to life. Apparently, this sordid use of science had been going on for some time, in secret.

She didn't like to think of him being imprisoned in a laboratory, with debriefings by MI5 the only relief. But she wasn't sure about him regaining the flesh; it was as if he wasn't really hers any more. Nevertheless she joined in the campaign and also wrote him a personal letter, bidding him welcome to the twenty-first century. She received a standard reply. A few months later, Napoleon was released to begin a new career as an advisor on French military history.

Then the buzz started. The University, encouraged by a grant from the European Government, awarded him an honorary doctorate in recognition of his post-resurrection services to the study of the era in which he was first alive (1769-1821). The quiet word was that France didn't want him, England didn't trust him, and Brussels had decided that the History Department of a Welsh University would be the place where he could be expected to do the least harm.

History and all its staff crammed into the interview room, eager to see the new Dr Bonaparte. Everyone acknowledged that the application process was a mere formality; his name was in the brochure and students were being recruited on the strength of it. Colleagues were just curious to get a good look at him, tickled by the idea of vetting such a celebrity.

He seemed remarkably well for a man who had spent nearly two hundred years in a tomb. True, the tip of his nose did have a squashy necrotic quality that was not attractive and his earlobes were in tatters. But never mind that, new body parts were being grown for him in labs all over the world. Bit by bit he was being restored.

His new eyes searched the faces of the History Field. He stared at Marjorie and looked her up and down until she blushed. Then he fixed his gaze on a point above her head. He said nothing. His tongue was still growing on the back of a mouse in Milton Keynes and wouldn't be delivered for at least another week.

Nobody spoke. Nobody was sure if he understood English. Nobody dared to mention the large gap in his CV.

Marjorie wanted him to look at her again. To 'catch his eye'. At which thought she began to giggle.

A storm of indignation raged across Napoleon's face. He pierced her with a look, pushed himself out of his chair and walked stiffly from the room.

They waited to see if the Emperor would come back; but he did not. After a few minutes they all trooped out after him.

Marjorie tried to apologise, but Napoleon refused her the opportunity. He did not acknowledge her if they passed on the stairs. There was silence at the photocopier. He had been given his own office and, since he no longer had a digestive system, had no need of the refectory. He was as far beyond her reach as he had ever been.

The Head of School told her, off the record, that Napoleon had marched in and handed over a letter of complaint. In correct but ambiguous English Napoleon stated that he was not used to being examined by a giggling woman.

The Head of School, relieved that he wouldn't have to speak French, presented him with a copy of the University's Equal Opportunities policy, smiled, bowed and showed him the door. Napoleon tore the document to shreds and threw the pieces down the stairwell.

He retreated to his office where he spent most of his time reading and learning how to surf the internet. He had a lot of catching up to do.

Marjorie tried to forget about him but it wasn't easy. He was so aloof, he seemed so arrogant, yet every time she met him she experienced a kind of emotional electric shock. She recognised in herself the classic symptoms of a woman in love: she emitted donkey-like guffaws of laughter whenever he was in the room; she attracted attention to herself by leaping from his path and tripping over her own feet; worst of all, she had started to ignore her friends – just like in a real relationship. She kept looking his way in case he was looking at her. Her heart groaned. Did he even have a heart? If only she could find something about him to despise.

Term began. Students flocked to Napoleon's classes, but his tongue had not been delivered on time – the mouse in Milton Keynes was weakening: tissue growth was slow. A Green Studies activist wrote an article in the student magazine, *Daff*, objecting to the exploitation of a small animal for the purpose of maintaining the Emperor's expensively embalmed body. He should never have been let out of the tomb. Was there a place for him in the classroom?

Napoleon's lectures went ahead as planned. They were well attended, despite his silence. He had his students read aloud from the commentaries he had written on Plutarch, Homer's *Iliad* and the life of Alexander the Great. He was interested in everything and refused to confine himself to his allotted area of history. Raiding the territory that rightfully belonged to his colleagues, he produced discourses on Industrialisation, the October Revolution and the Second World War. He began to write a novel.

While his words were read out in lectures Napoleon strode about the room; in seminars he wrote on the board and jabbed at it with a long stick, his face a playground of emotions. His students either loved him or hated him. Some were fascinated by his fiery glances and white gloves. Others were annoyed by his habit of tapping them sharply on the head if they weren't paying close enough attention.

The national press picked up on the mouse story. They ran daily bulletins charting the tongue's growth and the mouse's decline. Confrontations in the corridors between students who supported Napoleon's right to speak and those who supported the mouse's right to life threatened to disrupt the smooth running of the University.

At the staff Christmas party he was surrounded by hangers-on, eager to appear on close terms with celebrity. His formal uniform, complete with knee breeches and a rosette, made some people regret not having worn fancy dress.

Marjorie, repelled by the force of her desire to be near him, maintained a respectful distance. She observed him from the far side of the room. In the semi-dark his skin took on a pearly glow. He did not drink or dance. Marjorie danced to forget. Whenever someone bought her a drink she gulped it down.

By midnight the floor was wet with beer. One young technician slipped and collided with another. They grappled, each trying to get the other in a headlock. Oblivious to the scuffle, Marjorie swayed in a space by herself – until the fighting pair backed into her, knocking her down.

She looked up to see a pair of short legs in white satin stockings. It was Napoleon, standing with his back to her as if she were a barricade. He glared at the two young men and pointed with his baton at Marjorie. Sheepishly they separated and slid off to the bar.

Napoleon turned and bent down to offer Marjorie a hand. She dared not pull on his white-gloved fingers but held them gently while she scrambled up. Emboldened by drink, she decided not to let go until he did. Napoleon led her back to his table and made the others move up so she could sit beside him.

'Thank you,' mouthed Marjorie, for the noise was too great to allow speech.

'The pleasure is mine,' mouthed Napoleon in return. For the first time he smiled at her, showing his perfect new teeth.

At Christmas the mouse died. It made the evening news. Napoleon, who was in South America having his earlobes replaced, was warned of the possibility of trouble at the airport. He travelled incognito to Canada, where he picked up a new nose and some fingertips, before flying back to Heathrow on New Year's Eve. Marjorie volunteered to collect him. She had spent an anxious time alone, wondering if he would return.

His flight came in just before midnight and he was able to slip through customs while the demonstrators were singing *Auld Lang Syne*. On seeing Marjorie he dropped his attaché case, rushed forward and embraced her.

'Oh, Napoleon,' said Marjorie, 'I'm so glad you came back.'

He looked splendid. He turned his head to show off his restored profile and removed his gloves so she could admire his new fingers. She took his hand and examined it.

'Why, that's wonderful,' said Marjorie. 'I'm so happy for you.'

At the end of the long drive down the M4 she was supposed to drop him at his lodgings. But the street outside was filled with animal rights activists combining a sit-in demonstration with a New Year's Eve party. There was nothing else for it. Marjorie took him back to her place.

She intended to give him her bed and make up one for herself on the sofa, but he shook his head, indicating in mime that he had no need of sleep. He spent the night reading from her store of books. In the morning the floor was strewn with them. He made her a pot of fresh coffee and sat on the edge of the bed while she drank it.

In January the protestors turned their attention to the laboratories. A couple of car bombs later and the government began to wonder if Napoleon was worth the trouble.

One by one, research facilities all over the world were intimidated into halting their efforts to keep Napoleon and his kind intact. It was time to let nature take its course. The University wasn't pleased. He still had a year and a half of his contract to run. There were complaints that he was starting to take too much sick leave. 'He is technically still dead,' Marjorie defended him from her corner of the staff room.

The Head of School noted her special rapport with the Emperor and she was asked to make sure that he stayed as fit as possible. Part of her was pleased to have the chance to spend more time with him; part of her was alarmed at the responsibility.

She marshalled him to the gym and attempted to keep him

in shape. But without artificial regeneration he was, by early summer, decaying visibly. The new parts of him were wearing out quicker than the bits preserved by the embalming process. Marjorie decided he would have to give up the weights when two of his fingertips remained attached to the apparatus.

The doctor said that stress was accelerating Napoleon's decline so Marjorie took him to yoga classes. He learned to pretend to breathe in and out. He learned to go 'Hah!' and claw the air like a cat. It seemed to relax him: when the instructor said he had 'a tree' growing inside him Napoleon did not argue – he yawned. Marjorie saw his mouth open wider and wider, while his perfect teeth remained closed. When his jaw was open to its widest extent she held her own breath, afraid that his dentures would fall out and clatter to the floor.

By June he had lost the will to maintain bodily and mental integrity. He flopped in her office, wearing baggy shorts and displaying the lividity of his flesh. She had so wanted to be able to go on believing in him.

At the end of term he moved in with her; he needed someone to look after him. And so, in the evenings, when she should have been writing her paper on regicide, she allowed him to lie with his head in her lap. Lying down, he didn't seem as short. With the blinds lowered his skin didn't look so grey. His body cavities were as clean and odour-free as they had been for two hundred years. But his new nose was beginning to decay and even the students had started to complain about the smell it caused in the classroom.

He passed her a piece of paper on which he had written, 'I miss the passion, Marjorie. The rage of desire I can no longer feel.'

She stroked what remained of his hair. She knew exactly what he meant.

My Cousin's Breasts

My cousin Carole's breasts are huge. They sprouted when she was eleven and by the time she was fifteen they were really starting to get in the way. Carole blamed them for everything that went wrong in her life: she wanted to be a newsreader but the careers officer sniffed and said she *might* have a chance as a weather girl; she wanted to be a dancer, but her outsize boobies unbalanced the *corps de ballet.* Unlike me, she didn't have the washboard look, which is what it takes to look good in a tutu. 'It's all right for you, Natalie No-Tits,' said Carole. 'At least boys don't recognise you by looking at the front of your blouse.'

She was right, but then, they didn't seem to recognise me at all. What's the point of being able to pirouette if nobody asks you to dance?

We were close when we were younger, my cousin Carole and I; our mothers are sisters. We bobbed side by side in their wombs; we shared a midwife and delivery room at the local hospital; we were practically twins.

Carole was born just a few minutes before me, but in our early years on the outside, she didn't develop as fast as I did.

'Carole was the first to smile,' said my aunt.

'Ah, but my Natalie was the first to speak real words,' said my mother.

'Carole was the first to crawl.'

'Yes, your Carole was so good at crawling she didn't bother to walk until she was two. My Natalie had to keep stepping over her.' It was true. I was always ahead.

Carole had a lovely nature though. We all agreed on that. My mother said we should call her Treacle because she was thick, slow moving and really very sweet. But we never called her this to her face, or so my aunt could hear. Nobody wanted to hurt Carole's feelings. And nobody wanted to upset my aunt.

My mother and my aunt were devoted – to each other and to saying what was on their minds. This sometimes led to rows. But, as my mother reasoned, at least with Aunt Susan you could always rely on getting the truth. When she said she didn't want a second cup of tea she wasn't being polite, she meant it. When she said a dress made you look flat chested and anyway you didn't have the legs for short skirts, she wasn't being unkind, she was being honest.

Carole didn't have much to say about anything. She let me decide what games we'd play. Sometimes it was hard always having to be the one with the ideas. It was a big responsibility and it got me into big trouble at times, like the afternoon when we played hostage, and I forgot to untie Carole from the apple tree by teatime. She was crying and my aunt shouted at me, calling me a bully and a terrorist. My mother looked serious and sent me up to my room. But when I got a chance I told Carole I was sorry and in the end her mum made her buy me an ice-lolly to show that there were 'no hard feelings'.

So, yes, we were close – until Carole changed.

Carole's breasts, non-existent until our first year of secondary school, seemed to sprout, not overnight, but one September lunchtime in the playground. We were shivering under a luke-warm sun pretending that the summer wasn't over when her nipples just popped up under her shirt. I checked my own chest. Nothing. Carole saw me looking and glanced down at herself. We didn't say anything; we both put on our jumpers and looked the other way.

That Saturday we went on a group outing to the lingerie department. My aunt bought Carole her first bra; my mother bought me something labelled a 'skin-tone chemise'. It was a beige vest; we all knew. Carole looked at it, looked at what she was getting, looked at me. A new light dawned in her eyes. It was almost intelligence. She stood up taller. It made her tiny tits stick out.

Everyone thought it mattered to me, but it didn't. Not then. I wasn't in a hurry; the thought of acquiring body hair was too frightening. I'd seen my mother's inexpertly shaven armpits, the winter hairs she let grow on her legs to keep out the cold. They made me shudder.

But six months later Carole required cups. It was hard for me not to be overawed by her lace trims, her adjustable straps. I begged my mother to buy me something relatively bra-shaped, even if I didn't have anything to hide. 'But it doesn't matter,' said my mother. 'Don't be in such a hurry to grow up.'

She didn't understand. *I* wasn't in a hurry to grow up; it was Carole. I just didn't want to be left behind. Eventually my mother gave in and bought me something. It was beige, as usual, not much better than a cut-off vest. I was glad to have it, but found it surprisingly chilly to wear. I was cold on my belly and back where the rest of the vest was missing.

Carole showed me the red marks where her bra straps cut into her shoulders. It was a bit like breaking in new shoes, she said: all that rubbing in unaccustomed places.

My mother said, 'See? See how we women suffer?'

Not long after that I had my first period and found out what she meant. It wasn't just the pain and the mess and the turning white and the headaches. It was the whole business of sanitary towels. My mother wouldn't hear of me using tampons: I was too young. So, in the very moment of becoming a woman, I felt like I was being put back into nappies. In those days 'pads' were square-edged, thick and about as comfortable as having a brick in your knickers. They had a thin strip of adhesive down the middle. A great innovation, far better than belts and pins, apparently. But they didn't stick where they were put, did they? A good idea, yes, but under-developed. The system worked OK as long as you stayed still. As soon as you started walking, the pad was on the move too, climbing upwards over your behind to poke out through the waistband of your skirt. Running to the loo was a race against disaster. Better to walk, carefully, with your hands behind your back pressing on the thing to keep it in place. That's why some girls had days off school; they didn't dare go out.

I consoled myself with the thought that at least now I'd catch up with Carole. I started looking at myself sideways in the mirror, pulling my T-shirt tight. Now I too had nipples. But change was slow. I wasn't swelling as fast as I should. You'd think that sharing a gene pool with Carole would have given us some characteristics in common. Well, by the time we reached the third form it was clear that we were, physically as well as intellectually, quite different. Our academic achievements matched our cup sizes: As for me; Cs for Carole.

Yet Carole was always complaining. 'My neck aches,' she'd say, 'and my back. You don't know how lucky you are.' Then we'd go off to our separate lessons. We were in different streams by then: in the same form but not in the same class. I was heading towards the rock of university, Carole was navigating a course between hairdressing college and a degree in marketing.

When I felt bad about the way I looked I tried to be rational. I'd lie in the bath and look at my body as it lay under the water. I wasn't fat: but then I had no curves at all. Straight up and down and far too skinny according to my aunt. But what teenage girl, since the history of teenage girls began, has ever felt happy with her body? 'At least you know boys like you for who you are and not the way you look,' said Carole.

Daniel Stanton was one year and about a million miles above me. He had gorgeous hair and his eyes were brown. I had always thought about him, but now I began to think about him regularly and with some dedication. Whereas in the past I had found him easy to talk to, now I didn't know what to say when he spoke to me, my best effort in a six-week period being a mean-sounding, 'What do *you* want, Stanton?'

I usually tried not to think about him when I was in the bathroom (especially not when I was on the loo). But he was always around on the edge of my mind and it was easy enough to conjure his image in the steam above the bath.

The windows were dark and dripping on the inside. I wondered what it would be like to see a face outside the window: its nose, mouth and eyes blurred by the dimpled glass. Our bathroom was on the second floor, but there were such things as ladders and ventilation grilles and tiny spy-cameras.

I took to using bubble bath. One day, not long after, I found my first pubic hairs. I was doomed to be hairy *and* flat chested.

Reason told me I was better off than Carole now and in the long run: boys couldn't see past her tits; teachers treated her as if she couldn't possibly think *and* have bosoms that size (surely there was no blood supply left for her brain); other girls our age avoided her. They didn't want to be compared with Carole and found wanting. It made me sick to see the way boys ogled Carole and then sniggered behind her back. It was pathetic. They all wanted her but they had to make comments, as if they could get over *their* feelings of inadequacy by making *her* seem less worth having. The only boy who didn't act that way was Daniel.

I was avoiding him in person even though he was hardly ever out of my mind. I couldn't breathe when he was around. How would I ever be able to speak to him with no air in my lungs? And then something happened: he had his hair cut – ridiculously short. Younger boys started calling him Big Ears. He went all red, his ears reddest of all. I thought: no. And, just like that, he lost all his power over me.

Turns out I was glad. I really was. I didn't need to care any more whether I saw him or not. I even began to feel sorry for him because he had become so unattractive and unlovable. He was still a genuinely nice person. Just not someone you could imagine kissing. I would never let him touch me now that I knew what he *really* looked like.

One day, feeling sorry for him, I said, 'All right?' when our paths crossed. Amazing how easy it was.

If only his hair had not grown back.

By the time we did our mock GCSEs Carole had progressed to a 36 double D and tried out three boyfriends. They had all proved disappointing. Their interest was entirely focused on her anatomy. They had nothing to say and neither did she. Each encounter was made up of long, awkward silences followed by a pounce, which found her in no mood to surrender. For a time she embraced the idea of being single and independent. I was pretty good at that myself.

Daniel and I were on nodding terms. We rarely spoke but saw each other often. Tired of our long-distance nearly-romance (glances meeting across the crowded playground, or sliding together from opposite sides of the assembley hall) I worked out his timetable of movements and knew exactly when I might bump into him. On Mondays I'd be walking up the science wing corridor to my locker, with Carole in tow, before lunch, and he'd go by in the opposite direction towards the canteen, with a group of his mates. I could see them walking towards us through the glass panels of the swing doors which sectioned off the science wing. One day we all arrived there at the same time and Daniel, like a perfect gentleman, held the door open for us; only his mates barged through and we had to move out of the way. I knew their tricks. 'Bouncing off Carole' was a recognised and hilarious team sport among the boys that year. She stuck out her elbows like I had taught her, while I 'accidentally' did a bit of shoving back. Daniel just stood there, holding the door open until we were ready to go through. He smiled at me. He didn't look at Carole. He didn't stare at her tits. I smiled back at him.

Carole and I walked on a bit.

'He's nice, isn't he?' said Carole.

'That Daniel's a snob,' said Carole a week later. We were in my bedroom; my mum and hers were drinking coffee downstairs.

My cousin had burst in on me and caught me looking at a website dedicated to cosmetic surgery. I was thinking of asking my mum for a boob job for Christmas, but figured she'd probably make me wait until I was at least sixteen.

I clicked on the link for 'breast reduction' and said, 'Hey, Carole. Maybe this is what you need.'

Daniel wasn't taking any notice of her and she didn't know what to do about it. I smirked. Carole had been trying to catch his eye all week but each time we passed him it was me he looked at. He even went a bit pink himself. 'Maybe you're just not his type,' I said.

Carole thought about that for a bit. Then she said, 'What do you think of this?' Lifting her T-shirt she showed me her new bra. It was purple, covered in lace and made her boobs look like two large cushions. They were pushed up so high she could have rested her chin on them.

'Not so much upholstery, more a piece of furniture,' I said.

She pulled her T-shirt down again and lay back on the bed and sighed. 'Do you think I can get Daniel to notice me?'

'I thought you said you weren't interested in boys.'

'This is different. I really like him.'

'Oh. Well, you know, don't be too disappointed. Like I said, maybe you're not his type. Physically, I mean. Not everyone likes big boobs.'

'No?' Carole sounded doubtful.

'Are you two behaving yourselves?' my aunt shouted up the stairs.

'Yes, we're talking about sex,' I shouted back.

From then on Carole did all she could to get Daniel to notice her, aiming her tits at him like twin torpedoes. I was glad to see that he managed to evade them every time.

Not long before Christmas something marvellous happened. Daniel started walking me home from school.

He lived not that far from me but his quickest way was by a different route. So I knew something was up when I saw him ahead of me. I didn't know whether to catch him up or slow down. I decided to just go on as normal as if he wasn't there. But how hard that was.

He was there nearly every day. Sometimes he was ahead of me and sometimes behind. If Carole wanted to come back to mine I had to make some excuse. I didn't want her to know or she'd insist on walking home with me every night. (I thought she was getting quite selfish, only thinking about what *she* wanted. She never stopped to think that I might like someone or that someone might like me.)

It was nearly the last week of term before Daniel got up the courage to speak to me. I'd been disappointed to see that he wasn't around when I left school that day and I'd been looking out for him all the way. Someone came running up behind me. Another jogger? They could be scary with their sudden panting in your ear. So I turned just to check and it was Daniel. I turned away again. He slowed down. Oh no. Would he think I didn't want to speak to him? He must have been running to catch me up. I looked back again. He was stopping, out of breath.

'Hi,' I said and smiled.

'Hi,' he said, blowing air out when he should have been taking it in. We stood there. 'You know you shouldn't be walking home on your own in the dark,' he said.

'Oh, that's OK,' I said. 'I'm a big girl.' Wrong. In so many ways. Quick, say something else. 'But if you're going this way, we could walk together.' Too eager?

'OK.'

Easy. It felt natural, as if we knew each other. And we started regularly walking home from school together after that. We didn't start off together from school of course; the others would have made fun of us; besides there was usually Carole to get rid of. That wasn't too hard because she lived just close to the gate but in the opposite direction. And Daniel had to lose his friends too of course. But every evening, somewhere along the way, when we got to the quieter streets we naturally fell into step together. It felt right. Sometimes there were silences and I felt he would have liked to say more, but I knew it didn't matter. Things could happen slowly between us because they were going to go on happening. We had our whole lives.

Usually he said goodbye to me at the end of my road, under the streetlight. It was an orange light, unflattering, but never mind. If he could like me in that glare then how much might he love me by candlelight, or by moonlight? How he would gaze at me as we danced under the stars on our balcony in Tuscany, or on the deck of our sailing boat in the Caribbean or…

'Bye then,' he said.

'Oh. Bye.'

I went down the road to my house.

'Hi, Mum,' I shouted.

'Hi,' said my mum, coming out of the kitchen. 'Isn't your cousin with you?'

'No,' I said, taking off my coat.

'Only your aunt rang and said she isn't home yet.'

'Oh.' In fact, I hadn't seen her after school that day.

There was a knock at the door. It was Carole. She was looking at me and her bottom lip was trembling.

'Come on in,' said my mum. 'Your mum's worried about you.'

Carole said nothing; she went straight upstairs to my room.

'I'll ring home for you then, shall I?' my mum shouted up the stairs. She shook her head.

I took my time before going up. Carole must have seen me talking to Daniel. I didn't know what I was going to say.

'I hate you,' she said.

'Carole, love,' I said, sounding like my mother. 'It's not what you think. We're just walking home together.' But even as I said it I couldn't stop a grin spreading over my face.

The last day of term. In my bag, three things I might give Daniel: a red heart powdered with snow; a football card game, which was also a quiz; and a humorous Christmas card. I didn't know if I would give him all three or just the card. Or, if he gave me a present, I could give him the card game. Or, if he gave me a definitely romantic present, if he said he wanted to see me over Christmas, I could give him the heart. My own heart thumped in my throat when I thought about that.

He was waiting for me after school, which pleased me except that Carole was still there. We stood there awkwardly for a minute, the three of us, then Carole said, 'Shall I come round to yours? Mum's probably there.'

'Thing is,' I said, 'I've got stuff to do when I get in. And I think mum's gone Christmas shopping. See you tomorrow, I expect.' I gave her a smile and set off. I heard Daniel say goodbye to Carole. I didn't look back.

Daniel and I didn't say much on the way home. It was cold and I could see my breath and his. I changed my breathing so that we exhaled together, twin plumes. I wondered if Daniel was trying to decide, as I was, which present to give. Should I give them all? I wanted to speak but it wasn't the time to say anything ordinary. Anything ordinary would have been wrong.

We went on like this with the silence thickening, until we reached the end of my street where we stopped, as usual, under the glare of the street lamp. Lights like these, all over town, covered the stars with orange fuzz. This was it. I turned to Daniel and unclenched my teeth. 'I got you something,' I said.

'Oh,' he said. He looked startled.

'It's just a card,' I added hastily.

'I didn't get you anything.'

'That's OK,' I said, reaching into my bag.

'I mean, I haven't written my cards yet.'

'Oh.' I nodded, looking down at the ground.

'Sorry,' he said.

'That's OK.' I looked up and smiled brightly to show him everything was all right.

'Right.' He shifted from foot to foot.

He looked so uncomfortable I began to feel sorry for him.

And then he said, 'Umm, what do you think your cousin would like?'

'Pardon?' I said, blinking.

'Umm, your cousin Carole. What do you think I could get her for a present?'

I would have taken a step back but my heart, my real heart not the one wrapped up in my bag, had turned to stone, broken in two and sunk. I couldn't move.

'Yeah. Well, you know…' The words stumbled out of his mouth. 'If I get you something, I ought to… you know.'

'Know what?' My voice sounded sharp.

'Don't want her to feel left out,' he mumbled.

I took a breath. Then I smiled. 'Of course,' I said. 'Poor old Carole; she needs cheering up.'

'Does she?' He looked anxious.

'Well, you can imagine,' I said.

'Yeah?'

'Well, it's not easy for her, is it? People don't take her seriously. Most boys are only after one thing. You know.'

'Umm…'

'Your friends, they're just as bad.'

'Are they?'

'Yeah, always sniggering. You know it's got so bad she's…'

'What?'

'No, I shouldn't say.'

'OK then.' He looked relieved. He cleared his throat. He opened his mouth.

'Breast reduction,' I said. 'She's that fed up.'

'No!' He went pale.

'Oh yes,' I said, hitching up my school bag, turning my feet towards home. 'She's talked about it.'

He swallowed.

'It's not a good idea.' I turned back, leaning towards him. He leaned forward too. In a low voice I said, 'There'll be scars.'

'Oh.' He straightened up. 'Right,' he said, stepping back. 'Well…' He hesitated. 'You'll be all right now, won't you? Getting home?'

'Oh yes,' I said brightly. 'I live just down there on the left.'

And then he was gone, leaving me standing there, alone in that ugly light.

Stroking the Dog

'Dog massage?' said Jim. 'It's just a fancy word for stroking.'

'Well, I think it's a lot more than that and so do several other people whose opinion I admire,' said Betsy. 'Why don't you ever support what I do? I'm trying to do something good here.' She waved a handbill at Jim; he read it, to show how seriously he took her. There was a lot of stuff about health benefits, to the strokers as well as the dog.

'It's symbiotic,' said Betsy.

'You're turning this into a science? How much are they charging?'

Betsy shrugged.

'Why can't you do something normal?' he said.

'I miss Bruno,' said Betsy.

'He was just a mutt,' said Jim. Damn dog used to leave hairs everywhere, especially on the bed where he slept between them like a hot and heavy bolster. Betsy had cried an ocean when he died but Jim had just been glad he could go out at last without having to brush himself all over like he was leaving a shift in a gold mine. 'No one,' said Jim, 'should keep a dog in Manhattan.' After all, he was the one who went up and down in the elevator three or four times a day, who had to read all those signs shrieking: 'Curb your dog!'

It had been embarrassing when Bruno could no longer make

it to the park; he started doing his business just anywhere. Jim had to look the other way while the poor mutt tried to cock his leg and not fall over. And picking up dog dirt under the eyes of passers-by! Betsy wouldn't do it. All Betsy had ever done for the dog was pet him and feed him from the table and let him climb on the bed.

At the end, when Bruno couldn't hold it anymore, he stank, and made the apartment stink too. Then Betsy agreed he should be banned from the bedroom, but she kept to her side of the bed as if the dog was still there.

The trips up and down in the elevator became more frequent, but even so, he once pissed, when they were just on their way back up, and with a mournful look, all over the newly washed laundry of a lady from the fourteenth floor. Jim yelled and yanked the lead, but that only made the dog fall over and the lady cry out, 'Oh, please don't!'

Jim wiped up the splashes with a Kleenex and offered to re-wash the linen. 'He's an old dog,' he'd said, by way of apology. She'd nodded and said of course it was just an accident, but soon after that they got a letter from the Committee saying something must be done.

'It's him or us!' said Jim.

Now here she was, aiming to pay over good money to learn how to massage the canine species. It was all nonsense – he was sure of that – and wouldn't last. Still, if it gave her something to think about.

'There are all kinds of things to consider,' said Betsy, excited after the first lesson. 'You have to get to know the client: he or she may have arthritis, or painful old scars from fighting…'

To pass her course Betsy had to get in so much practice. 'We are not getting another dog,' said Jim. She wouldn't need to, said Betsy; she would massage the homeless ones.

But it seemed there was a boom in dog massage and a shortage of dogs needing it. People in parks were getting offers from students who wanted to practise on their pooches. Stray dogs found themselves being petted, fed and passed around.

There was an epidemic of canine caressing. Some people, even some dog owners, thought it was all going too far.

'The dogs aren't complaining,' muttered Betsy to Jim at the Public Meeting. By then she was working as a volunteer at the pound. 'You don't see them biting the hand that strokes them.'

A man stood up, identified himself as 'an ordinary dog-lover', and suggested proposing a new law to prohibit the therapeutic massaging of dogs in the city without a licence.

'But where do you draw the line between ordinary, casual, spontaneous contact and serious intentions to heal?' said a woman.

Without getting to his feet, Jim cupped his hand to the side of his mouth and said loudly, 'When they stop calling it stroking and start talking about *effleurage*.' Betsy hit him on the arm and looked away, red-faced.

To get enough practice, Betsy ordered a blue rubber dog from a catalogue supplied by her training course.

'Is it a dog or a bitch?' asked Jim as he watched Betsy go to work on Bluey's shoulders.

Betsy wouldn't answer.

They were probably asexual, thought Jim, a fact he ascertained later: no realistic orifices. Even the mouth was sealed and the eyes closed, with a little furrow between them as if the dog was working through its pain.

'If I were a dog would you stroke me?' said Jim.

'Don't be disgusting,' said Betsy.

Betsy talked of setting up a charity when she qualified, to provide dog massage for people who couldn't afford it. 'I'd like to call it CHUM,' she said. 'Short for Canine Healing and Massage.'

'That's CHAM,' said Jim. 'You know, I'm thinking of starting a charity myself. I'd call it SAG. That's short for Stroke a Granny. Just think of all the poor old ladies out there who can't afford that kind of therapy.'

Betsy ignored him. She set up a stall near the subway on

72nd Street and got people to give donations. Bluey went along for demonstration purposes. Jim lurked behind her chair, not wanting to leave his wife alone in a city full of nutcases. Besides, it gave him a chance to eyeball the ladies who stopped to admire Bluey and even pat him on the head. He was amazed to see how many people gave money.

Hanging about on the street had its compensations: 'I wouldn't mind stroking them puppies,' he muttered under his breath, as a smiling girl with bouncing breasts walked by.

'Don't be disgusting,' said Betsy.

Girl on a Pedestal

The editor of the *Buckington Bugle* is worried about my tendency towards broadsheet, big-city cynicism. 'Stop trying to be Julie Burchill,' he says. 'This is a local paper; end of story.' Apparently my review of the Brownies' Christmas concert has upset some parents.

Where did I go wrong? After all, I had faithfully reported the enthusiasm of family members: vying for camera angles and clapping loudly; but I had also added – unforgivably, as it turns out – my own opinion, calling the choice of material 'unoriginal and yawn-inspiring'. I think this was justified when you consider that the high point was a shaky rendition, sung in the round, of 'Campfire's Burning' for which the lights had been dimmed to heighten the effect of seeing half a dozen timid little girls clustered around a stack of twigs with a red light underneath. It was exactly the same set-up as when I was a Buckington Brownie, nearly thirty years before.

'People aren't interested in what you think,' says the editor. 'The job of the art critic in this town is to describe what's on offer and reflect what people are saying about it.'

He makes it clear that I will get one more chance.

But do I care? Do I care whether I'm a success by the standards of this small-town paper? I've been away long enough not to mind what people think of me, and I'm back here for my own reasons. I'm not exactly looking to fit in. If I want a social life I can head up to London for a weekend; no, I'm here to write my own work, if I can. It had seemed like a good idea to work for the local paper while I was doing it, that was all. With my track record as a freelance, I thought they'd be glad (and lucky) to get me.

Not so. My editor was grudging, making it clear that I would have to prove my worth.

So nothing has changed in my home town. Twenty years ago, when I left school with no idea of what I wanted to do, except write, I sent a letter to the *Buckington Bugle*, asking if they would take me on. There was no reply and I went elsewhere, halfway around the world and back, gradually building up my freelance portfolio. So I knew I could support myself. It was just that I thought this job would be easy and regular and leave me plenty of time for my higher purpose: finishing my first novel.

'I'm going to send you on one more assignment,' he says, 'and if I don't like your piece then I'll pull it and write one myself. If that happens, don't expect to get any more work.'

He's sending me to the arts centre to interview the two young people responsible for a new exhibition: 'Girl on a Pedestal'.

'Hannah Gifford is a local girl,' says the editor. 'Not long out of art college. Her parents are farmers, well liked and well connected. Don't be too critical. It's probably rubbish, but remember: it's not just about the work.'

'So how do you want me to approach it?' I say.

'Find out what the public thinks,' he says. 'Give us the view of the majority. That's what they want to hear; that's what sells newspapers in this part of the world.'

'I am an Installation,' says the girl, 'and this is Stew.'

They sit together, on a table, side by side, Hannah and Stew, looking out at me with grey moody eyes through identical jagged black fringes.

'Are you brother and sister?' I ask.

'No,' says Stew, taking Hannah's hand.

Hannah has long straight hair and pale skin; she is petite but well made; she is…

'Aren't you going to write that down?' says Stew, meaning, I assume, Hannah's portentous announcement, not my own wayward thoughts.

I look past him, round the gallery space where Hannah will give her performance, or show her art, or install herself, or whatever it is she thinks she's doing. It is a wide, square, white-painted room with tall arched windows; they let in plenty of light. No furniture except the table. No sign of a pedestal. Nowhere, even, for me to sit down. So I stand and face them and repeat dutifully: 'I am an installation,' nod a few times, then ask, 'In what way… exactly?' My pencil noses the paper, as if anxious to take down a reply. Stew looks up at the ceiling and sighs. The ceiling is a very long way above our heads.

I shift my weight and try again. 'Is it possible to tell me what exactly *is* going to happen?'

Hannah developed this work at art college: 'I showed this as my final piece,' she says. 'But it's more important for us to do this, to show it here.' She waves her hand at the otherwise empty room.

'Right. So… ' I waggle the pencil from one to the other, 'which of you is the actual artist?'

Hannah blushes.

'It's a collaboration,' says Stew.

'But who had the idea?'

'Actually,' says Hannah, shaking the hair out of her eyes to look at me directly, almost defiantly, 'I did.'

My next question – 'How do you feel about showing your work to the home crowd?' – is intended to be a little more sympathetic. I've been away and come back myself I tell them; it's a small town.

'Oh yeah,' says Hannah. 'You know, I think my dad said you went to school with him.'

'Really?' I say. 'Who…?'

'And anyway,' says Stew. 'Hannah's not ashamed of who she is.'

'So, how do you think people will remember you?' I ask.

'As talented,' says Stew.

But exactly what they're going to do or show, neither of them will tell me. They're 'not into talking about it'.

'At college,' says Hannah, 'I wrote that it was an allegory of the effects of time on a psychosomatic-social being.'

'But that's just art college bullshit,' says Stew. 'We can't *explain* it. You just have to *get* it.'

I smile as condescendingly as I can and say, 'Isn't that always the way?'

An hour later, with all the blood in my body pooling in my shoes and my tongue sticking to the roof of my mouth, I stagger across the road to the Boar's Head.

What I like about the Boar's Head is that it hasn't changed much from my under-age drinking days, before college, London, New York: other lives. Its walls are perhaps a deeper shade of cigarette-tar brown, but the same oil-painted ships still battle choppy seas inside their picture frames and the smell – of wood steeped in the local beer, soggy carpet and fags – is for a moment or two as magical as when I was sixteen.

'What can I get you?' It's the very same landlord, older of course, as everyone is in this town. There's nothing like coming home to remind you how you're aging.

Seated on a stool at the bar, and having taken the first restorative gulp of gin and tonic, I look at my notepad: Hannah Gifford; twenty-one; a potential graduate of Diffington Art College; local girl. I'll have to find more to say than that. It's tricky. The exhibition opens tomorrow but the actual opening night, when 'the whole thing goes interactive' as Stew put it, is on Thursday. By then the paper will have gone to press for its Friday distribution.

'What about a last minute update?' I'd asked my editor.

'To be avoided at all costs,' he says, 'though in an absolute emergency you can ring me, and then email it in, by midnight at the latest.'

Which means I will have to write my review article before the exhibition 'goes live', disguising, as far as possible, the fact that I haven't seen it. It would have been in their own interests for Stew and Hannah to tell me what is going to happen, but they don't seem to think it's necessary.

'Word of mouth is the best publicity,' Stew said. I decide he's right. Before I reach the end of my drink, I've formed a plan: drop in to the exhibition every day and hang about listening to what people say about it; that way I can't go wrong.

I toast this resolution and down the last of my drink in its honour. Having decided I had better not have another, I am about to leave when a man comes up to the bar, gives me an eyebrow flash and a don't-we-know-each-other smile, and says, 'Hi'.

Now, this is what happens when you come back to your home town: people you've quite naturally forgotten pop up and expect to be remembered. The ones who know you from primary school are the worst. You struggle to shrink the bloated features before you to the memory of some nub of a boy who once punched you on the arm or pulled your hair when you were six to show he liked you.

So I just blank him, and slide off my stool, as planned. It isn't until I get outside that I realise two things: one, though he looks familiar, I can't place him – I don't remember him from school; and, two, he is the best-looking man I've seen since I came back.

Driving home, I dismiss him from my thoughts: no point regretting another opportunity wasted; I would just remember to do better next time. Instead, I think about Hannah Gifford and the fact that I knew her father.

Gordon Gifford: I remember his first name because he suffered for it in the seventies, when 'Gordon is a moron', that line from the song by Jilted John, pursued him round the playground of our comprehensive school. But what did he look like? There is only one clear visual memory of him lodged in my mind, relating to an incident way back in primary school, when Gordon's illicit use of a ballpoint pen, and his persistent chewing of its top, left him with ink all over his mouth and chin. He looked like a blue-blooded boy who'd been punched in the mouth. I remember the look of confusion on his face as he tried to work out why his chin was wet, and the fleeting thrill I felt, wondering if he would actually be poisoned to death in front of me, or merely disfigured for life with a blot of indelible blue.

Neither had happened, obviously, because here was Hannah, his only daughter, all grown up and ready to show the world what she's made of. Literally, as it turns out.

Hannah is naked; or would be if she were not wrapped in cling-film. The effect, against the white walls, is of fragmented water. Leaning forward a little on her pedestal, which is also painted white, she looks as if she is up in the air, but going somewhere. Or she looks like a mummy in a hurry, wrapped in transparent bandages; or an ethereal speed skater.

She does not move. When I first see her, I can't help but think of those mime artists that pose as living statues. In particular I remember a clown who would drop his trousers and raise his wig if a child (it was always a child) toddled up and put a small coin in the hat at his feet. But at Hannah's feet there is no box for taking money, nor does she respond when anyone walks into the gallery or makes some comment on her work or her appearance (these being, to a great extent, the same thing).

Whispers are amplified, distorted and then lost in the high-ceilinged room. Low voices sound more urgent than the words that are spoken justify, as they seem to make the walls vibrate. What are they saying? Mostly they are being very nice, so as not to upset Hannah. A few people enter with children and take them away again quickly, though there is not a nipple or a wisp of pubic hair to be seen. I suspect it is because they know the children may say potentially embarrassing and true things and ask awkward questions, such as, 'What is that lady doing?' – to which neither the parents, nor I, would feel qualified to give an answer.

Still, the visitors do come. Word has got around.

On Monday, Tuesday and Wednesday, I visit the gallery in order to spy on people's reactions. To disguise my intentions, I sit and appear to be listening to Judy, the volunteer in charge of the table at the door. The exhibition is free, but Judy smiles at the visitors and informs them that they might like to make a donation. They also have the opportunity to sign a sort of visitors' book. In fact, this is an A4 ruled sheet on a clipboard, with space for name, address and comment.

Judy sits with her back to Hannah and I sit at right angles to Judy, so that I can see the whole room, while pretending to listen to her waffle. Despite my best efforts, I find myself knowing far more about Judy and her life than I would like: I learn of her adventurous cats, the squeak in her washing-machine that sets her love-birds chirping in a competitive manner, why one should never groom a horse while wearing cashmere. I am having difficulty keeping my eyes open; it is a struggle to tune Judy out and focus on the hushed comments of the visitors as they circle the Girl on the Pedestal. Luckily, as the week progresses, there is a tendency towards more forthright opinion.

'How silly!' says one elderly lady, using the right to free speech they issued with her bus pass. 'What is the world coming to?'

To Hannah's credit she does not react. I wonder how long she will stand there without a break. Hours, as it turns out. When she wants to get down she simply straightens up, stretches and jumps to the floor. When she wants to get back up she borrows Judy's chair.

How does she manage to pee, I'd like to know. I would ask her but she won't speak to me, and I do not wish to invade her privacy to the extent of following her to the Ladies. I do hang about in the corridor, however, and through a crack in a door leading to an office, see Stew, sitting in front of a computer monitor. I knock and go in.

'What's up, Stew?' I say.

He says 'Hi' and leans back in his chair. He's looking at a screen showing the gallery. I hadn't realised the whole exhibition was being videotaped. 'Is this part of it?' I say. 'Or is it just for security?' You know how worked up people can get about art.

While I'm looking a man comes into the gallery and looks around. I imagine he's thinking: 'Is this it?' Leaving Stew, who is biting his nails, I hurry back upstairs.

On the desk Judy is oddly quiet. The man is prowling round the empty pedestal. Again, I have the feeling, as I did with the man in the pub, that his face is familiar. Another good-looking fella. Hallelujah. Pity he's interested in this stuff, though he keeps looking over at me. When Hannah comes back, she breaks silence at sight of the man. 'Dad!' she says. 'What are you doing here?'

So that's it. This is Gordon Gifford. This is what he looks like at forty – unrecognisably handsome without a trace of blue ink.

But he has no time to answer because people are clumping up the stairs and Hannah has to get back up on her pedestal. She grabs the chair I was about to sit on and carries it over. Gordon offers her a hand up but she bats it away. Once in position she shoos him off, and he picks up the chair and brings it over to me.

'Here,' says Gordon to me. 'Have a seat.'

'Don't we know each other?' I say.

'Do we?' says Gordon. 'Oh yes.' He runs a hand through his hair, distracted. 'Of course.' But he says nothing else and goes to stand by the wall as the group comes in.

What do I expect – some declaration that he has loved me all his life and never been able to get my youthful beauty out of his mind? Hang on; he's married anyway, isn't he? So let him wait over there, arms folded, scowling at anyone who stares too long at his daughter.

Uncomfortable in his presence, the group – a family of tourists in shorts – does not linger. We hear them giggle and exclaim as they go down the stairs.

'Dad,' hisses Hannah, when this group has gone. 'Go away.' It appears she is embarrassed. Looking at Gordon's body language, I would say the feeling was mutual and that, besides this, he considers her to be somehow in danger.

Gordon comes back every day, but shows no inclination to talk about old times. Just as well, as I would perhaps have felt a little awkward if we had become chummy. My review of Hannah's work is, on the whole, unfavourable. In the circumstances, I cannot take both pieces of my editor's advice. In this case, faithfully reflecting public opinion precludes me from appearing neutral.

The comments generated by the exhibition are overwhelmingly either bewildered, as in, 'What?' and 'I waited for ages for something to happen', or decidedly negative. 'A bad case of Emperor's New Clothes' is a line I intend to quote. For me it sums up Buckington's considered response.

Judy has been persuaded to provide me with photocopies of the comments sheets, in case my editor, or anyone else, requires proof that these are not my own words. I do also mention, of my own volition, that large numbers of people have attended, and I use the words 'brave', 'audacious', and 'avant-garde', because I find it rather touching that anyone could think of making a living with such rubbish. Hannah is, I'm afraid, like so many others before her, just playing at it, even if she has chosen to do this in a most difficult and embarrassing manner.

Every day she stands there, motionless, for far longer than an artist's model would have to endure. She does not complain, neither does she waver. Such strength and dedication are admirable, but why is it any different from sitting, or standing, on a pole, or living in a glass box for forty days? That isn't art; it isn't even magic. Perhaps it is spectacle. That is all I can say.

On Thursday evening, I attend the 'Interactive Opening', having spent the day writing and rewriting my copy. In the end my editor accepts it despite the negativity of its tone, because I have shown him the comments sheets. I rejoice in being able to offer him the views of the majority.

There is quite a queue to get into the arts centre, headed by Hannah's father. Gordon manages a pensive nod. I confess I am a little disappointed that he doesn't seek my good opinion, but I gather that he does not care to have it, either for himself or for his daughter's work. Something else is troubling him.

I do not have to wait in the queue, of course, but can go right in – except that I am locked out. Reduced to knocking, I am further embarrassed when the door is opened a mere chink and I find myself being scrutinised by a fierce woman I think I recognise.

'Press,' I say, holding up my pass.

'I know who you are!' barks the woman, acting out her role of guard dog. Of course she does. The recognition is now mutual and complete, though I don't know her real name and can't quite bring myself to address her as Brown Owl in this context.

'Can I come in?' I say.

'You *can*,' she says, 'but whether you *may* is another matter.'

Oh, ha ha. 'I'm expected,' I persist.

'Well, nobody told *me*.'

'Nevertheless.' I push the door and slide through. Once in, I ignore Brown Owl and sweep upstairs.

I'm surprised to see someone I know in the gallery. It's the handsome stranger from the Boar's Head, the one with the familiar, but unplaceable features. Judy is there too, twittering on, something about money (the soaring cost of birdseed, probably), but I manage to evade her.

'Hi,' I say to the handsome stranger, taking care not to call him that to his face. 'We sort of met the other night.'

'Oh, yes,' he says. 'Aren't you the art critic?'

I wonder how he's come to hear about me. Does he mean 'the art critic for the *Buckington Bugle*' or 'The Art Critic'?

'What do you think of it?' he says.

'It' isn't actually happening at this point. The Pedestal and the Girl are hidden behind what looks like a white shower curtain.

'Well, it's different,' I say, brightly, not wishing to make 'cruel' the first impression he has of me. Or the second. His first impression, thinking back to my behaviour in the pub, was probably 'unfriendly'. I smile again, hoping to obscure that thought.

Just then the doors open and we part to let people through, though not without a look at each other that promises future conversation.

When the room is full, music begins to play, a tinkling, mechanical tune, such as you might hear from a musical box, very like the theme tune to *Camberwick Green*.

People stop murmuring and wait expectantly. Slowly, slowly, the shower curtain rises, like a white shroud, pulled up by a rope running through a pulley attached to the ceiling, unsheathing Hannah's cling-filmed form, posed as before. Her father is standing very close, as if he's afraid she might fall. Most people here have seen her already. I wonder why they've come back for more.

The music changes to a fanfare of trumpets and Stew emerges from behind a white screen, dressed in a white fencing outfit and carrying a foil. It is painted black, and this, together with Stew's dark hair, stands out against the white walls, so that as he walks, head and sword seem to float.

As he approaches the pedestal he swishes a few cuts of the foil. 'Ooh,' says the crowd, moving back. Gordon goes into a crouch. Stew, in a classic lunge, leans forward and pushes an invisible button with the tip of his foil. As the pedestal begins to revolve, so Hannah comes to life. She looks bewildered, then, seeming to notice how high she is above the ground, falls to her knees, gripping the sides of the pedestal. Stew goes back behind the screen. Gordon stands up again, glancing anxiously at Hannah. Stew reappears with an axe.

His intention, I presume, is to take the axe to the Pedestal, not to Hannah, but he doesn't get a chance to swing it once, as Gordon puts a hand on his shoulder, which seems to have the same effect as a Vulcan death grip. Stew crumples to the floor. Hannah says, 'Da-ad!'

'Blimey,' says someone. 'Is this all part of the act?'

On the whole I'm sorry I haven't been able to report the whole fiasco. I suppose if I was really keen on the job I would revise the story and email an update. However, I feel my original words will not only be justified, but seem lenient and forbearing in the circumstances. Besides, there has been no death to report: Gordon and Stew have been parted and the axe taken into custody. Hannah has left in what looked to me like a sulk. I have plenty of material for next week's column. Besides, I'm keen to catch up with the mystery man.

I see my stranger talking to Judy and spot my opportunity to rescue him and earn his undying gratitude.

'Have you met our new patron of the arts, Nathaniel Green?' Judy says. 'I was saying to you earlier; he's buying the exhibition.' She would say more, but people are moving towards the doors. 'Duty calls!' she says, and excuses herself to go stand by her collection box and offer audience response questionnaires.

Now I remember where I've seen him: in the newspapers. He's a big collector, one of the biggest. What he says, sticks.

'Mr Green,' I say, 'how can you?'

'Nathaniel,' he says, 'or Ned; my friends call me Ned. You mean the practicalities of staging the work?' He frowns and looks into the future: 'Hannah will be exhibiting at different times of year and in different venues, to be arranged. Long term, I can see what you mean; she'll get older. Well, that will be interesting too, don't you think? And besides, I'll hold the franchise.' He brightens up now. 'I could have exhibitions in countries around the world. Say, would you like to join me over the road for a drink?'

I go with him, gladly, to the Boar's Head, and find myself with the opportunity to sit on the bar stool I slid from the first time we met. Taking up this position again, I bestow upon him my full smiling attention.

'The possibilities are endless,' he is saying. 'You know, one of the things they might do is flay a layer off her, so that it hangs, like skin...'

'What about her father,' I say. 'Is he going to turn up at every event?'

'It makes for good publicity,' he says. 'But if it became a real issue we could even use a different Girl. It might not have the same energy, but I guess we could do it.'

'And may I ask how much you're paying for it?' I say, which, if you consider my job, is hardly a rude question.

'More than enough to create a great deal of interest,' he says. 'In fact, I think Gordon will see things differently when he's had a sight of the cheque his daughter's getting.'

I hesitate then say, 'I wonder if a negative review would bring the price down.'

'Don't do me any favours on that score!' he says, looking surprised and a little pleased. His eyes search mine, as if he wonders whether I am joking. 'I know not everyone's like you. They won't get it straight away. But you know a big price attracts attention.' He leans in closer. 'Between you and me, I don't need to make the money back; it's more important to back something I believe in; but I don't see why I'd lose money on this one. Did you see the number of people there?'

He kindly refrains from pointing out that the *Buckington Bugle* is unlikely to have much effect on world opinion.

'I guess she's become a local celebrity,' I say and glance over his shoulder at the bar clock. It's ten to nine. 'We finished early,' I go on. 'Do you think people got their money's worth?'

'Why don't I tell you over dinner?' he says.

'I'd love to, Ned,' I say. 'But you know what? Could we make it tomorrow?'

'I understand,' he says. 'You probably have a deadline.'

'Yes,' I say. 'Yes, I do.' I write down my phone number, swallow my drink and get down from the stool. Unsure whether to kiss him on the cheek, I stick out my hand; he takes it and pulls me towards him. Our cheeks touch and kisses whisper past our ears. With an apologetic look, I pull away. 'Sorry,' I say, 'but you know how it is.'

'Oh yes,' he says, putting his hand on the seat of my vacant bar stool. 'I know: a deadline is a deadline.'

The New Adventures of Andromeda

'Help?!' calls Andromeda. No reply. The sea idles at her feet. She drums her fingers on the rock to which she's been chained for the best part of three hours. During this time neither monster nor hero has appeared.

Two-hours-and-fifty-seven minutes ago, Andromeda had been feeling quite attractive, having spent most of Thursday preparing for her appointment with her designated hero, Perseus. She'd carefully rubbed the hairs off her legs with a well-soaped pumice stone; she'd bathed in goat's milk (and after milking fifty goats she'd needed to); she'd rinsed and oiled her hair. Andromeda was hoping that Perseus would make her a present of Athene's mirror, the one he'd used to defeat the Gorgon. She was hoping he'd descend from the sky, using the winged boots Hermes had given him, or astride Pegasus, that beautiful white winged horse born from the damp earth soaked in the Medusa's blood.

Two-hours-and-ten minutes ago, even without a mirror, she'd been able to look down and approve of the way the sea spray was curling her perfumed hair and making her dress cling damply to the contours of her body. She'd even considered the possibility that she might glance at the Gorgon's snaky head and turn herself to stone. After all, she would never look more lovely.

After two-hours-and-fifty-nine mirrorless minutes – it is by now well past the hour when she should have been commanding a servant to crack open the first amphora of the day, and sinking into her lover's embrace – she feels, not lovely and vulnerable, but bedraggled and venomous. Her chilly flesh is taking on a mottled aspect and, with the incoming tide lapping round her ankles, she can't help reflecting on the fact that, since no one else cared to, she'd had to fasten her own chains.

A grey, scaly boulder, no longer able to keep still, shifts an inch or two to the left and lets out a groan.

'Come on out!' yells Andromeda. 'You might as well.'

The sea monster gets up from his crouch, rubbing the calf of his hind leg. The face he pulls is terrible, but this is mainly due to cramp. 'He's late,' grumbles the monster.

'*You're* telling *me*?!'

'What do you think's gone wrong?'

'How should *I* know?' says Andromeda, whose nose is cold and could do with a wipe. 'I'm just the virgin.'

The sea monster rolls his eyes.

'You'd better be careful,' says Andromeda. 'For all you know he could be here right now. Don't forget he's got that helmet Pluto gave him. It makes him invisible.' She allows her eyes to slide past the monster's shoulder as if there is something behind him and has the satisfaction of seeing him duck and turn.

'Yes,' says the sea monster, 'I've heard that he's favoured by the gods.'

On cue, up clatters bare-chested Perseus on a horse; he holds the reins in one hand, in the other he carries a writhing sack.

'Quick,' hisses Andromeda to the sea monster. 'Hide.'

'Can't I cut straight to the menacing?' the sea monster hisses back. 'It's just that I'm awfully late for bathing my youngest.'

'Oh, very well,' says Andromeda. It means losing her moment alone with Perseus, but never mind. In her present mood, she'd find it hard to utter a cry of welcome and gratitude. Indeed, she feels rather inclined to bite his head off herself, but then where would she be? All alone and chained to a cold, wet rock, that's where. Right now, she wants her dinner more than anything. She hopes Perseus has booked somewhere decent.

'Where are your wings?' Andromeda can't help asking as he reins in his horse. 'No wonder you're late!'

The sea monster shifts from foot to foot as if hoping to be introduced.

'Get on with it then,' says Andromeda, crossly.

'I've always admired your work,' says the sea monster.

'Thanks,' says Perseus. 'And I've heard a lot about you.'

'I mean get on with the menacing and the killing and the rescuing,' says Andromeda. 'I'm catching a chill.'

'Charmed,' says Perseus, flicking her a look.

'Sorry.' The monster bows, apologetically. 'I'd like to chat, but the sun is sinking and it's a long swim home…' So saying he raises himself on his hind legs, roars and unsheathes his sabre claws.

Andromeda screams.

Perseus, instead of drawing his sword, looks thoughtful. He hooks the sack with the Gorgon's head in it over the pommel of his saddle, and gets out his diary. 'Well, as it happens it would suit me to reschedule. I had an oaf to see to on the way over and it took rather longer than I thought.'

'What?' says Andromeda.

'By the way…' Perseus leans forward and beckons the sea monster closer. The sea monster advances, keeping a wary eye on the hero's sword. Perseus, bringing his mouth close to the holes in the side of the sea monster's head where the ears should be, whispers, 'Who is she, exactly? I seem to have lost my notes.'

The sea monster sighs and recites impatiently: 'Her name's Andromeda. Her mother bragged she's more beautiful than Neptune's daughters.'

'And is she? I mean, after all, once one's rescued a girl I believe one's supposed to marry her and to be quite honest,' he glances over at Andromeda who grimaces back, 'she doesn't seem to have much idea of, you know, *grooming*.'

'Of all the nerve,' explodes Andromeda. 'You should have seen me *three hours* ago.'

'That's true, actually,' says the sea monster. 'You *are* rather late.'

'Indeed,' says Perseus straightening up and shutting his diary with a snap. 'And now if I don't hurry I'll be even later for my next appointment. Tuesday at three. Don't keep me waiting.' He spurs his horse inland.

'Great,' mutters the monster, trudging into the sea without a backward glance. 'And he promised to introduce me to that woman with the snakes.'

'Well don't imagine *I'll* be here,' shouts Andromeda.

The key is in her girdle and she reaches it easily, but her numb fingers let it drop into the water. She reaches out with her foot and is momentarily distracted by its puckered aspect. Just then a wave lifts the key up by its ribbon and draws it a little further off.

Andromeda bites her lip and gazes out to sea. 'Help,' says Andromeda, weakly at first. And then, much louder, 'HELP!'

The monster humps his back and dives for the ocean floor. Inland, the dust kicked up by the hero's horse is beginning to settle. The sun is sinking. There is no one else in sight.

Scary Tiger

Have you ever had an impulse? Standing on a railway platform have you never felt the urge to give someone a little shove?

In my lunch hour I'm waiting to cross the road to the baker's when I see a pregnant woman on the other side, also waiting. Woman as vessel; form dictated by function; baby-wrapping. I cross the road one way; she the other. We pass in the middle. Her eyes slide over me and away. She's thinking about danger from traffic, not me. Perhaps all she sees is a shape to avoid.

As soon as I see her I want to run across and punch her in the stomach. I *know*. I can hear you; I know what you're thinking. Please understand: I don't really *want* to, but I thought I might.

I suppose some people will assume I'm jealous. Or unnatural. I can hear the voices. Not *hear* them, you understand. I don't want you to think that I'm really *hearing* voices. But they play in my mind. Home movies.

I just had the thought and saw myself doing it. Her – doubling over, falling to the ground; old people stopping, gaping, shouting. Me instantly slashed in two by the knowledge of what I had done; what people thought of me.

You're evil, say the voices. This is exciting for them. They're like a restless audience, easily bored. I'm haunted by the people in the cheap seats; they won't shut up.

I've had all sorts of jobs.

The old lady watches me weigh the potatoes. I know just how many spuds make up a pound. I haven't converted to metric and neither has she, although the scales are set to kilos.

I smile a lot at the customers. This one smiles back.

She checks the change in her purse. Her hair needs washing and I think, she doesn't do it herself; she goes once a week to the hairdresser's; she'd like to go twice a week if she could. Still, she knows she's lucky, counts her blessings. Some of her friends can only manage once a fortnight.

Careful with herself. Lovely soft old-lady skin. Pearl-coloured ear-studs, not too big. A shade of lipstick rosy-pink. Blue eyes, fair eyebrows. Her hair should be white but she has it tinted strawberry-blonde. Pity it looks so stiff. She should wash it herself and forget the setting-lotion.

'Do you swim?' I ask her.

'Oh no, I never learned to swim.'

'You could still learn now,' I tell her. 'My mother learned when she was fifty-seven. It's never too late. It'd keep you fit.' It could liberate that hairstyle. At first she'd wear a swimming cap then one day she'd forget and maybe she'd get her hair wet and she'd borrow someone else's shampoo and start a conversation in the changing-room and maybe make a new...

'And can you do me half a cucumber?'

We have a lovely sharp knife for the cucumbers so the least amount of juice is wasted. I smile. 'Of course.'

If she knew what went on in my head. A feeling breaks inside me like a wave of cold sewagey seawater. If she knew. She would drop her fruit and run.

I let it all out in a sigh. I don't want to hurt anyone. Really, I don't.

How did I get to be like this? I'll try to think.

I remember being about twelve and at school and doodling on the side of my rough book. Among the spirals and stars and swirls that look like ferns unfolding, the word HELP yells up from the margins, so loud I wonder someone doesn't hear it and come rushing to my aid. Underneath my long-sleeved blouse my wrists are scratched red-sore.

The teacher is moving down an aisle on the far side of the class. She walks up and down between the desks for the whole forty minutes, talking and waving the good conduct book, or bringing it down with a smack on someone's head. We are like white mice glued to our chairs. We quiver, but cannot run.

My parents are never in when I come home from school. But that's no reason to want to kill them; in fact I'm glad they aren't there.

The carpet in the kitchen is new. In front of the sink and cooker it is covered by a new strip of tough see-through plastic. When will it be time for the plastic to come off? Never.

I'd get a lot of sympathy (and the house) if my parents die in a hideous car crash. The hill we live on is very steep. But I don't do anything; I don't know how to do it without getting caught.

When I leave school I cheer up a bit, and even more when I leave home. In fact, I become so cheerful, people remark on it. My boss expects me to be more serious.

'Hang on,' I say, and go out of his office and come in again, trying to look grave. But it's no good. The grin on my face is bigger than ever. 'I can't help it,' I say, melting into laughter.

Everything makes me laugh these days. I'm wildly in love with my boss. It's a happy love, uncomplicated, my secret. I know I could get someone younger and better-looking but he's nice and secure and undemanding and the fact that he's older and uglier than my 'standard' makes me feel thin and pretty and magnificently young.

I loved him then. But one day that love was used up; I longed to shed the useless weight of it, to shake him off. Is this how a murderer feels? One day loving, another day wanting to slice the no-longer-loved one out of your heart? Some people deserve to be eaten by tigers.

I don't feel right at all; I'm snarling. Even though I hold on to my outer expression, the face that's meant to put you at your ease, I'd frighten you if you looked deep into my eyes: I know I would. You want me to help you pretend the world is a nicer place? My little chats will make you think I care; I'll help you push back the darkness; all those awful things that happen. Don't worry, that can't happen here and now. Not to us. Squeeze your eyes shut and hang on; hang on tight to the merry-go-round.

So now I work somewhere else. It doesn't matter where; it isn't interesting work and neither are the people. I doodle on my telephone pad but I don't write 'help' any more. People would think it strange.

At the end of the long day, when the others leave together, I'll go to a bar on my own and stand there at the counter, drinking, rubbing my wrists and pretending, or not bothering to pretend, that I'm meeting someone.

Anything to put off walking to the station, that moment when I'm waiting in the crowd for the train.

Harvest

Michael pulled up outside Vanessa's flat in a shining four-wheel drive.

'Oh, my God!' said Vanessa, as she struggled to climb up into the passenger seat. 'When did you get this?'

'Well,' said Michael. 'We *are* going to the country.'

'We do have roads in Dorset, you know.'

She didn't say anything else for a while, which left him free to concentrate on getting out of London. Once they were on the M3, Vanessa said, 'You don't have to spend money to impress my parents.'

'I just want them to see that I'm taking this thing seriously.'

'This *thing*?' said Vanessa.

Without taking his eyes off the road, Michael reached across and squeezed her hand. 'Come on,' he said, 'the you-and-me thing. I know how important your family are to you. I want them to like me. I want them to know that we're prepared to go down at weekends; and they can come up to us.'

She bowed her head and spoke through a blonde curtain. 'Daddy doesn't much like London, but mummy might like to get away sometimes.'

Vanessa's mother had been an actress, her father a Commander in the Royal Navy; they were not rich, but somehow managed to live in a large house overlooking the sea. In Michael's mind's eye they lived a grainy black-and-white existence, somewhere between *Brief Encounter* and *The Cruel Sea.*

'Had many girlfriends, Michael?' the Commander was saying, in Michael's head.

'I won't deny I've lived the bachelor life.' He must try not to sound too defensive.

'And what's so special about my daughter?'

How could he explain? Michael had not understood love before he met Vanessa. Love, and the way it made his old friends behave when it hit them, had seemed an odd kind of practical joke that some of them simply refused to acknowledge as such. One by one his bachelor friends had slipped into coupledom; some were sheepish about the way they changed, others shrugged it off. As far as Michael could see, love made them do things unnatural to their bachelor souls and he had enjoyed telling them so. But after Michael met Vanessa a crowded address book seemed suddenly worthless. He found himself saying that life had been 'empty without her' – and meaning it.

All the way to Dorset Michael held a conversation in his head with Vanessa's father, rehearsing his responses until the Commander, satisfied at last, clapped him on the back and shook his hand, saying warmly, 'You're a man after my own heart, Michael. I felt the same when I met Vanessa's mother. It was in London during the Blitz…'

'Get ready!' said Vanessa, sitting up. Hours and miles had passed and they were now on the last stretch of trunk road before their descent into country lanes. 'It's a sharp turn at the bottom of the next hill.'

Just as the view on their left opened out all the way to the sea, Vanessa said, 'This is it!' Michael just managed a glimpse of green fields and dark woodland, church towers, clustered farms and the faraway shining water, before they plunged between the hedgerows of the Bride Valley.

In between directing him through lanes and villages towards the sea, Vanessa exclaimed over all the things she could see from her high seat in the four-by-four, her voice bright with excitement. 'Nearly there now!' she cried, as they swung out onto the main coast road and climbed the first hill. At the top, they seemed to hang a moment; the western half of Lyme Bay opened out below them; large in the distance were the yellow-faced cliffs: the flat top of Golden Cap, the slope of Thorncombe Beacon – those sea-bitten, green-backed hills. Beyond these, Lyme Regis, banked up to face them on the coast, the long slope of Black Ven, and shadowy headlands, stealing away into Devon. Michael was about to impress Vanessa with his geographical knowledge, gleaned from studies of the Ordnance Survey map and several guide-books, but Vanessa was leaning to the window and saying, 'I can see the house!'

Down a pot-holed track between fields they lurched, towards a line of trees standing parallel to the long shingle bank below. Through thinning leaves Michael could see the outline of a big square white house. Now he had a view that encompassed the whole of Lyme Bay, with the Island of Portland away to the east like a gigantic long-tailed sea beast head-butting the mainland.

Vanessa wound down her window and in blew salt air and the smell of seaweed, grass and reeds, tough pasture strewn with sheep's droppings, damp and dirty wool, with an acrid top-note of smouldering leaves. A stoop-shouldered old man, prodding at a bonfire with a rake, looked up and stared at them as they passed. 'I didn't know you had a gardener,' said Michael.

'We don't,' said Vanessa, and she leaned out and called to the man, 'Hello, Daddy!' as the four-wheel drive rolled past, its gleaming paint a shout in the muted landscape.

Vanessa's father raised a hand and began to walk towards the house. Michael drove round to the front and pulled up on the gravel. Now that he could see the house more clearly it appeared to be more grey than white, its render pockmarked and patchy. As soon as Michael had applied the handbrake, Vanessa jumped out and ran back to embrace her father.

Michael busied himself getting the bags out of the car, but when Vanessa and her father, arms linked, came round the corner of the house, he went to meet them.

The Commander gave him a searching look and held out a grimy hand. Michael took it, making sure to use a firm and manly grip. 'Steady on,' said the Commander, wincing. 'Mind the arthritis.'

Michael dropped the hand at once, only then noticing the outsized knuckles and the way the fingers slanted, like thorn trees do before the wind along that coast. He began to splutter an apology but the Commander said, 'That's our Vanessa. Always the same. Sink or swim.'

Just then an upstairs window opened and a voice fluted, 'Vanessa darling!'

'Mummy!' called Vanessa, and she darted into the house. Michael looked up just in time to see a plump woman in a flowery silk *peignoir* turning away from the window.

'Good drive?' said the Commander, looking at him with narrowed eyes.

'Oh, yes. Thanks,' said Michael. 'What a fantastic place this is. Such stunning views.'

'Glad you like it,' said the Commander. 'Well, I'll see you at supper; best not to leave the bonfire unattended, even in this damp weather.' And he went, leaving Michael standing outside the house with the bags.

Michael picked up two of them and approached the wide front door. He was about to call out a hello, when a robust-looking red-cheeked woman with black hair and dark eyes appeared, wiping her hands on her apron. 'You must be Michael,' she said. 'I'm Mrs Brightwell. If you'd like to follow me I'll show you to your room.'

'Oh, thank you,' said Michael. 'I wonder where Vanessa's got to.'

'I don't suppose you'll catch sight of her now till dinner-time. She'll be up with her mother.'

'Shouldn't I go and say hello?'

'Bless you, no. You'd better not. Her ladyship's not dressed for visitors and she's sure to keep Vanessa with her. Asking about you, I expect.' Mrs Brightwell gave a comfortable laugh. 'You'll see them both at dinner.'

Her ladyship? Michael stopped at the threshold of the house and put down the bags. 'Just a moment,' he said. Going back to the car he fetched three bottles of champagne. 'To help celebrate – umm, Vanessa's mother's birthday.'

Mrs Brightwell said, 'How lovely; we'll enjoy these I'm sure. I'll get them in the fridge just as soon as I've settled you in.' And she put the bottles down in the hallway and instructed him to leave Vanessa's things there too.

The house seemed pleasingly proportioned, its entrance hall spacious and its staircase wide. As Mrs Brightwell led him towards it, he looked around for clues: there was a hall table with an old leather dog lead on it and an empty silver tray that had not recently seen polish. At the bottom of the stairs was a large photograph of a man recognisable as a younger version of Commander Clifford, standing in shirtsleeves and cap on the deck of a submarine. Further up were photographs and then portraits of seafaring Cliffords of the past. Down the long corridor Michael felt he was being weighed up by the ancestors, a succession of men in wigs and white stockings, and ladies in pink satin dresses, with black dogs at their feet and square-rigged ships on the horizon.

'You're in the Blue Room,' said Mrs Brightwell, opening the door. Indeed it was blue, from coverlet to walls, though the carpet was badly faded and even threadbare in places.

In his room there were no portraits, only more pictures of sailing ships and a large print of the 'Raft of the Medusa', so placed as to appear to be heading out of the window and towards the open sea.

Michael put away his things, then lay down for a while, listening to the sound of waves booming on the shingle bank, until Vanessa came and knocked on the door. 'Why are you hiding up here?' she said. She smiled at him, then went to the window to look out. 'You have one of the best views,' she said. 'We only put important people in this room.' Michael got up and went to her, put his arms around her and kissed her. She leaned her head against him and he breathed in the scent of her hair.

'Come on,' said Vanessa, taking his hand. 'We mustn't keep them waiting.'

'Bubbles, what a treat.' Vanessa's mother sipped her champagne, raised her glass and looked at him with dark eyes. 'Thank you, Michael.' In her grey silk she looked like a seal with breasts.

He smiled and raised his glass. 'Happy birthday, Mrs Clifford.'

'Oh do call me Doatie,' said Vanessa's mother.

Doatie, thought Michael. Must I? Vanessa's father was staring at him again. What should he call him? Sir? Commander? Daddy? No, definitely not Daddy.

Vanessa smiled encouragement and he wanted to smile back and stretch out his foot under the table in search of hers.

Stop right there. What if he found the wrong foot? The thought brought him out in a sweat.

The table was certainly impressive: large faux pearls glowed on old white linen, silverware – clean silverware – winked in the candlelight; long-bodied silver animals were placed beside each plate. Michael had a dog, Vanessa a mermaid, the Commander a big fish, Mrs Clifford a peacock with folded tail. The fifth place – there had been no mention of another guest – was a bear on all fours. Vanessa rested the tip of her knife-blade on the back of her mermaid, as if she did so absentmindedly, then looked at him and smiled. He smiled back to reassure her; of course he knew what to do!

While Vanessa asked her mother about the arrangements for the harvest supper in the village, Michael and the Commander eyed each other. Michael thought he saw a hint of loathing swim in and out of the other man's eyes. A salty fire spat and crackled; piles of driftwood steamed upon the hearth, giving off a faint odour of sewage.

The Commander shifted irritably in his seat and said, 'Where's Mrs Brightwell with the fish?' and moved as if to get up.

'Don't fuss, darling. She'll bring it when she's ready.'

'Are we expecting someone else?' asked Michael, nodding at the unoccupied chair.

'Well, there's Mrs Brightwell of course!' said Vanessa's mother.

Michael went red and was opening his mouth to apologise, when the door was thrust open and in came Mrs Brightwell with the fish.

'There you are, Mrs Brightwell,' said Vanessa's father. 'We were beginning to think you'd been eaten by sharks.'

'Stove's playing up, Commander. And I see the fire in here's not chucking out too much warmth either.' She looked balefully at the hearth, before uncovering the platter to reveal a large whole sea bass on a bed of tough-looking greens.

'Champagne, Mrs Brightwell?' said Vanessa, casting Michael a look.

Michael hastened to fill the housekeeper's glass.

Mrs Brightwell received the glass and raised it. 'Here's to the birthday girl,' she said, and took a swig.

They all raised their glasses and drank.

'How kind you all are,' said Mrs Clifford. 'Shall we admire the fish?'

'It's a fine fish,' said Mrs Brightwell.

'A magnificent fish,' Michael put in quickly.

'A fish fit for a queen,' said Vanessa.

'What sort of fish is it?' asked Michael.

'A big one,' said the Commander, picking up his knife and fork. 'Now, will you be doing the dishing, Mrs Brightwell?'

While Mrs Brightwell was leaning forward to work on the fish, her rump obscured Michael's view of the Commander. So he turned to Vanessa and her mother.

'Was it caught round here?' said Michael.

Mrs Clifford smiled, but it was busy Mrs Brightwell who answered. 'The Commander caught it yesterday. Bit of luck eh, Commander?'

The Commander said, 'Mrs Brightwell likes to tease; don't you, Mrs Brightwell? Fish like this don't swim past every day.'

'A bit like our Vanessa,' said Mrs Brightwell, lifting some fish-meat clear of the bone. When she handed a plate to Michael, he thanked her and put it down in front of him. She handed him another and said in a low voice, 'Pass this along, would you, Michael? There's a dear.'

When they were all served, Vanessa said, 'Michael's all set to lend a hand with the harvest, Daddy. He's bought himself a nice new Barbour and a shiny pair of wellies.'

They laughed and Michael joined in.

'The fish is superb,' he said.

'And how do you like your sea kale?' asked Vanessa.

'Interesting texture,' said Michael. 'I've never had it before.'

'Grows on the shore,' said the Commander. 'I'll show you when we go fishing.'

After dinner they sat for a spell in the drawing room, which was chintzy and stoic. The walls were lined with bookshelves and a stack of hardbacks held up one end of a chaise longue. Michael sat next to Vanessa (not holding her hand) and asked things about the area, and about the house, all the time braced and ready for a return volley of questions; questions which did not come.

At last the Commander stood up.

'Early start tomorrow then, Michael,' said the Commander. 'Wake you at six?'

Michael laughed politely.

'He thinks you're joking, Daddy,' said Vanessa.

Michael couldn't sleep. He sat on the edge of his bed and stirred the fluff on the worn carpet with his bare big toe. Through the silence in the house, he could make out the flump and drag of waves on the shore.

He got up and cautiously opened his door. He hadn't even had a chance to find out where Vanessa was sleeping; so now he was just listening, hoping to be able to hear her voice and home in on it.

He could hear faint sounds of activity coming from below. Michael put on his new slippers, wrapped his new dressing gown over his new pyjamas, tied the belt firmly and crept downstairs.

First he went back into the drawing room and looked for something to read, something mildly entertaining. There were books on gardening and the gathering of edible wild plants, back to back with novels by Jack London and Iris Murdoch, mostly old hardbacks with tatty dust jackets. The book he really needed – *Getting on with the Cliffords: an Instruction Manual* – being absent, he passed over *The Call of the Wild* and picked up a copy of *The Sea, The Sea*. Then he went along the passage to the kitchen, knocked and pushed open the door.

Mrs Brightwell and the Commander were sitting opposite each other at the table. Between them was a white saucer holding some purple sludge. Their heads were close together and they both looked round as he came in. The smell in the kitchen was both tart and sweet. A big saucepan sitting on the stove was making gentle plopping sounds.

'Just wanted a drink of water. Got myself a book. Hope that's OK,' Michael said, moving quickly to the sink. He looked around for a glass but all the work-surfaces were clear.

Mrs Brightwell pressed her hands down on the table as if about to push herself up.

But the Commander placed one of his hands over one of hers and said, 'Sit down, Vera. There are glasses in the cupboard to your right, Michael. Help yourself. Mrs Brightwell's had a long day.'

'The jam won't set,' sighed Mrs Brightwell.

'Oh dear,' said Michael.

Silence.

'Well, goodnight.' Michael took the water and went back up the stairs. In the corridor he looked at all the doors and listened as he walked past. Nothing.

Back in his room, he read, until the sound of the waves dragged him down, at last, into sleep.

The Commander woke him at dawn with a cup of tea.

Michael went down to the kitchen to find Mrs Brightwell

stirring the contents of her vat with a purple-stained wooden spoon.

'Help yourself to porridge, Michael,' she said, nodding at another pan. 'And have a dollop of this.' She held up her spoon and the dark preserve ran off it. 'I still can't get it to set.'

The Commander came in and rested a shotgun against the wall. 'Rabbits first, I think, Michael.'

'I've never handled a gun,' he said.

'The main thing,' said Mrs Brightwell, 'is not to get in front of the wrong end.'

'It's better with two of us,' said the Commander. 'I usually have to make do with you, don't I, Vera?' They both laughed.

Michael wondered if he would have to shoot. Could the Commander's fingers pull the trigger?

'Yes,' said Mrs Brightwell. 'We used to have a dog; but then, rather carelessly, it died.'

The Commander's arthritic fingers had no trouble managing a shotgun. He was fairly silent at first, letting the gun speak for him. When enough beasts had been killed and collected and Michael was festooned with game, the Commander began to speak about Brandy, the foolish gun dog who'd got in the line of fire. 'Terrible waste. And you'd think she'd have had it in the blood. Worst of it is we shan't get the chance of a puppy for a good six months.'

On their return they found the kitchen empty. Michael stood while the Commander unhooked the rabbits and pigeons from his shoulders.

'Coffee for the hunters,' said the Commander. He made it himself then left Michael alone in the kitchen, while he took a tray upstairs to his wife.

The stove hissed. Moments passed before a door banged and Vanessa came in carrying a basket of mushrooms. He got up to take it from her; it wasn't heavy.

'Look,' she said, 'a parasol. And there was the most enormous puff-ball I've ever seen, but it had gone spongy.'

'Vanessa,' said Michael.

She took the basket from him and set it on the table. 'Don't worry,' she said. 'You're doing fine; just be yourself.'

Just then Mrs Brightwell busied in with an armful of wood, slammed it down next to the stove, said, 'Now then, you two,' and bustled out again.

Michael's voice dropped to a whisper. 'Actually, I think your father's getting used to me; he was telling me all about Brandy.'

That afternoon, the Commander set Michael to work in the garden. Michael had to be shown how to lift potatoes from the soil, a task the Commander clearly regarded as something every schoolboy should know.

Michael filled the sacks, working the garden from side to side. But he always seemed to be at the wrong end of a row whenever Vanessa went past. His back ached and he wanted to hear her say a few words of encouragement. The fourth time she went out with her basket she waved and smiled. He stood as upright as he could and waved back, grimacing.

He went on lifting potatoes from the soil with the fork, and bending to gather them, for what seemed a very long time. But he had to admit that it felt good to be outdoors on this quiet, white-skied autumn day.

Mrs Brightwell came past with a plastic box full of red and blue-black berries, followed by the Commander wiping on his trousers the soil from some carrots he had pulled.

Mrs Clifford, like an afternoon ghost, appeared at her bedroom window, wrapped in the same *peignoir* as yesterday. She waved at Michael, smiled and moved out of sight.

The Commander hauled away the full sacks of potatoes. His ancient trousers were smeared with soil and dried blood, to which clung wisps of rabbit fur.

Late in the afternoon Michael and the Commander went down to the sea.

They walked down across the fields in silence. Michael had put on his new wellies and Barbour. The Commander, dressed in an old jacket and sea boots, had looked him up and down and grunted.

Both men carried a rod and a bucket. Michael was expecting that now would come the questions – about his job, his background and his prospects – and he had his answers racked like sardines ready for the grilling. When they got to the shingle bank the Commander pointed out the source of the sea kale they had eaten the night before. 'Blanch the stems,' he said. 'See the way we heap the shingle up around them?'

A wooden bridge took them across some reed beds through which brackish water seeped. A short distance away was the car park at West Bexington and they crossed a track smothered by large pebbles, only suitable for horse or tractor, or going on foot. The Cliffords' old rowing boat lay behind a clump of bushes growing out of the shingle. Michael helped the Commander to turn it over and then they lifted it together and began to carry it between them, up the pebble bank.

As they topped the rise Michael felt the sea-wind and saw the whole curve of the Bay. Nearer the car park, the sea's edge was dotted with fishermen standing at the shoreline or seated behind rods perched on stands. Some had made encampments: tents, foldout stools, windbreaks, fires or portable barbecues. A few children were fishing with their fathers, and there were one or two women; mostly the females were well wrapped up, and reading, sitting on rugs with their legs stuck straight out in front of them, looking up now and then at the view. Michael and the Commander marched down to the water's edge, their feet flicking up pebbles.

At the lip of the sea the beach dived under the water, which was, on that day, deep and clear from the very edge. Here they set the boat down and, while the Commander held onto the stern, Michael climbed in and took up the oars. Then the Commander stepped on board, pushing with his foot to set them going. 'Easy today,' said the Commander. 'Hardly any swell and the tide's just right. Just row straight out until I tell you to stop.'

Michael rowed. The Commander rubbed his gnarled hands together. After a bit he said, 'That'll do. Don't want to end up in France.'

The Commander showed Michael how to bait his hook and cast his lines. They settled down to fish. Michael faced the shore; the Commander had his back to him. Again there was silence between them. Perhaps it was another hangover from the war, thought Michael, a case of 'careless talk costs lives'. But that was nonsense, if you worked it out. Vanessa's father would have been a boy still in 1945.

'I was shipwrecked on a desert island once,' said the Commander. 'For quite a long time actually. Very hot. A real *desert* island. Not much water. Best to keep your mouth closed when the sun's up, conserves moisture.'

Michael nodded, but then remembered the Commander couldn't see him, and said, 'Oh?' But there was no reply.

It was the Commander who reeled in the first three catches. Michael wanted to reel in his line too, but there had been no pull to suggest he had a bite. Long minutes passed and Michael wondered if he could bring up the subject of his intentions towards the Commander's daughter. But he didn't know how to begin. His fingers went numb but he did not like to blow on them. Why hadn't he thought to wear gloves? Time stretched out and snapped back on him so that he actually jumped when the Commander spoke again.

'Getting a big chilly. Time to have a bit of a row, go out and check for prawns,' said the Commander. He began to reel in his line.

'Prawns?' said Michael, hastily following suit. 'Fantastic. I love prawns.'

'These are good ones,' said the Commander. 'Big and juicy.'

The Commander took over the rowing and brought them out to his marker. Then he hauled on a line that dipped under the surface of the sea. Michael looked over the side, as well as he could for fear of tipping the boat.

'Ah, here she comes,' said the Commander. 'Lend a hand. Take the oars and keep the boat steady.'

Reaching out over the side with a gaff hook he drew something big and heavy through the water towards him. When it was up against the boat he leaned out and began to gather large prawns and drop their living bodies into the bucket between his legs.

'This can be your contribution to the harvest supper,' said the Commander. 'If you're staying until tomorrow?'

'Oh, yes,' said Michael, 'well, that's very kind.'

'Good man,' said the Commander. 'Right then. I suppose to make it honest you ought to do some of the harvesting yourself.' And he pushed the bucket over to Michael, who looked at the prawns in it – at their semi-opaque yellowish little bodies, their spindly black eyes like a tangle of old-fashioned pins, and their suckery little mouths.

'Here,' said the Commander, pushing the big thing through the water in Michael's direction.

Michael looked over the side. Coming towards him was the bloated and partially decayed carcass of a once-black dog. The tails of the prawns still attached to it swayed in the currents round the boat.

'Wonderful,' said the Commander. 'Bounty of the ocean. You look a bit pale, Michael. Are you all right?'

Michael felt the boat heave.

'Waste not, want not, Michael,' said the Commander. 'I'll hold her and you pluck.'

Michael had no intention of eating them. He felt mean about giving them to the villagers but consoled himself with the thought that really there was nothing wrong with the prawns; of course there wasn't. But still, just in case, he pretended he had been called back to London on urgent business. To his relief, Vanessa agreed to go back with him.

'What a shame you'll miss the harvest supper,' said Mrs Clifford.

'Yes, isn't it?' said Michael.

Vanessa, Mrs Clifford and Mrs Brightwell were all very impressed with the catch, and gave their men due praise. The

Commander grinned at Michael, who managed to smirk sheepishly back.

As he went to his room before dinner, he looked again at the paintings and photographs of the Cliffords, with their succession of sad-eyed labradors, and hoped they were not able to judge him from beyond the grave.

Michael knew his visit had been a success when he was hailed with cordiality and warmth as soon as he showed his face that evening.

'Well, we're very pleased to have met you,' said Commander Clifford. 'A pity you can't stay longer, but no doubt you'll be back again. We can't do without our daughter, you know.' He looked fondly at Vanessa then raised his glass as if to seal the bargain.

'Anyway. Here's to the hunters,' said Vanessa's mother.

They all smiled and drank; Mrs Brightwell took the lid off the large dish in the centre of the table.

'You brought back so many of these beauties,' she said, 'we thought the village could spare us a few for tonight. No reason why you should miss out altogether.'

She held out her hand for Michael's plate and gave him a large helping of prawns, and a brilliant smile.

'How marvellous,' said Mrs Clifford.

'Yes,' said Mrs Brightwell. 'Dear Brandy. She goes on serving.'

They all laughed, and Michael joined in, nervously.

The Commander took a prawn, peeled it, and popped it in his mouth. Vanessa and the others did the same. With her mouth full, not chewing yet, Vanessa looked at Michael, waiting like the others.

He picked up a prawn and held it in one hand. With the fingers of the other hand he pulled off its head. Shucking the body from its case, Michael brought the lump of pink flesh to his mouth – and put it in.

Vanessa smiled, her mother nodded, Mrs Brightwell winked.

'Good man,' said the Commander.

Then they all began to chew together.

The Real Thing

A red light burns on the altar: this is the eternal presence of God. What would happen if I crept up there and tried to blow it out?

Father Treavey coughs inside the confessional box. I don't think he has germs; the cough means, 'A-*hem*. Is anybody there? Or can I go home for my tea?' A nice Saturday afternoon tea with sandwiches and homemade cake.

I get up off my knees, bob up and down before the altar, cross myself, and go into the box.

'You'll have to speak up, my child,' says Father Treavey, 'I'm afraid I can't hear you.'

Kneeling in the dark. His face, looking away on the other side of the grille, as if I see it through a dark veil (I wore a white one for my First Communion, that's how I know). I also know what he looks like: a face with the colour rubbed away, leaving it pale, soft, pouchy. A vague, polite smile.

I begin again, but louder, 'Bless me, Father for I have sinned. It is one week since my last Confession.'

'Dear me, my child,' says the priest, in a tone of the mildest shock. 'A whole week. And have you sinned again already?'

'I have, Father.'

'And what have you done in the last week to be sorry about before God?'

'I've...'

'Yes...?' I see him tilt his head.

How to begin?

It was a long hot climb up from the playground, and I was panting by the time I reached the top. My sister Debs was sitting with her back to me. Her friends, Molly and Karen, must have given her a look to warn her, because Debs said, without turning around, 'Go away.' The boys with them didn't look at me.

I sat down.

Debs snorted. Molly said nothing but rolled her eyes. Karen said nothing but adjusted her bra, giving rise to a little flutter of hands from my sister and Molly, as if they would like to adjust their bras too. Except they weren't wearing any. The boys looked at each other and grinned. Karen laughed her little spluttering laugh; my sister and Molly went pink.

I looked away. Below us on the field, a group of girls were making outlines of houses using cut grass and wondering where to put the bedrooms (I *told* them they had to make bungalows); further down, a bunch of my year were playing their favourite game.

It used to be *War*, in which one group of grey shorts and skirts swooped on another and there was some shirt pulling. I wouldn't play; *War* is evil, isn't it? Unless someone is really wrong and you are right. I told them that. It didn't make any difference: they just played without me. The whole school played, except the little ones. But then Michael King got stung in the face with nettles and it was nearly his eyes.

Next thing, I thought, they could be hitting each other with sticks. That really worried me, so I did what I'm supposed to do if I'm worried. I told the nearest grown-up, which was the dinner-lady, and she told the headmistress, who gave the whole school a stern talking to and said that *War* was banned.

So now my year and some of the older ones too, I see, were playing a game called *Rape* instead, which is a bit like kiss-chase, with more wrestling. I wasn't asked to join in.

'What are you doing?' I said, half-looking at my sister; but the question mark hung there for all of them.

'*Nothing*,' said Debs. 'Go a-*way*.'

Then the bell rang and they all went down the hill, nobody saying anything.

Sunday. Debs and I set off for Mass together, as usual. In her short brown skirt and patterned blouse my sister looked like she was going to a disco.

Mum was still reading the paper when we left.

'Why don't you come, Mum?' I said.

'Too much to do, honeybunny. But you go and say a prayer for me.'

I always do; I think I do all of mum's praying for her, but I don't mind. It's better than having her roast in Hell. I know, mum isn't a Catholic, so for her it's not really a sin to miss Church, like it is for me; and she keeps the promise she made when she married dad to bring us up 'in the faith', even if she didn't keep the one about forsaking all others (as dad says). I think that, in her way, mum is a good person. But still, I can't help worrying about her immortal soul. 'It's great being a Catholic, Mum,' I tell her, and I really believe it.

'Why's that, honey?' says my mum.

I have to think; it's always been a feeling; now I have to find words for it: 'Because you never have to be on your own.' But after I've said it, I wonder if it sounds stupid, because she smiles.

When we got to Hangar Lane, which is only half way to the church, Debs says, 'You go on. I'll catch you up. Wait for me after.'

'But where are you going?' I said.

'I've just got to speak to Karen,' she said. 'Don't be nosey.'

I walked on a bit; this was wrong. I turned back to see if Debs was watching me, but Karen was already there and they were talking and not looking at me. Then, to my amazement, instead of saying goodbye to Karen and coming after me, my sister turned away with her friend and went off in the opposite direction. In a few moments they had turned left down the steep short lane to the kissing gate and the meadow by the river.

I closed my mouth and swallowed. A car came past and the woman driving looked at me with a frown. Instead of turning and walking to the church, I followed my sister. I would have to miss Mass too – **and that was my first sin.**

When I got to the top of the lane, Debs and Karen were not to be seen, but the kissing gate squeaked and banged. I hurried down after them, but stopped before going through.

On the far side of the gate was an old man in a flat cap, shuffling along the path, tugged by a little white dog at the end of its lead. He was a big man, so the dog had to work very hard; it was panting and its tongue stuck out. Walking away from the path, towards the riverbank, were Debs and Karen – and Molly was there too, and behind them were three boys, Michael King and his mates. The man stopped and turned to look at them. His mouth opened and he shouted, in a much louder voice than I expected: 'I know what you're doing!'

Michael King turned to look at him and I ran, scared, back up the lane and waited and waited, until the little dog, half-strangled, pulled the muttering old man up the hill and away.

Hurrying back to the meadow, I opened the kissing gate slowly – just a little bit, so that it gave just a tiny peep – and slipped through. My heart beat so fast I felt sick. There was no one to be seen in the meadow. Trying to go quietly, but not look as if I was creeping, I went along the path, all the way to the other side where another gate, flanked by tall dusty nettles, leads into the North River housing estate. Then I turned round, thinking if I ran all the way to church, I would only miss the start of Mass. But what about my sister? I didn't want her to get into trouble.

Not knowing what to do, I was thinking I might cry for a bit, when I heard Karen laugh from over by the river. Of course: the grassy bank slopes to the water and you can't be seen there if you're lying down. Then my sister shrieked.

I pulled the sleeve of my Sunday cardigan down over my hand and bent a big nettle stalk near the roots, trying to snap it; but it wouldn't break. I had to pull the whole plant up by the roots. Trailing soil, I charged the riverbank. But they weren't there.

A 'Ssh' and a giggle and an 'Oh!' came from behind the tresses of a willow tree.

As I crept up I could see the boys' knees and shoes and the girls' bare legs where the fronds hung thinner near the ground. They must have seen my shoes; someone said 'Shit!' and there was the sound of a gasp and a zip.

I parted the fronds. All six were there: I did not much notice the others. All I could see was the front of my sister's blouse – undone – and that Michael King sat next to her and had his hand in his lap and something pink and fleshy in his hand. It twitched and I shouted at them all, but especially my sister, telling them what I was afraid of: 'Don't you know that God is watching you?'

It's funny. Sometimes you say something and when you first say it you really mean it; it's what you really think, but then, when the words are out there, twisting around in the free air, you get to have a good look at them and then you wonder: why do I think that? Is that such a good idea?

Debs says I am weird; I don't think she is being very kind, considering I told a lie to mum to save her; that is, when mum asked how Mass had been, I said, 'Good,' – which might not have been a lie, only I knew it made her think we had been to church.

So later in the week when she said dad wanted to know why we *hadn't* been to Mass on Sunday (how would he know? He doesn't go either), mum sat me down and gave me a serious talk about how I didn't need to lie and I could tell her anything and how much it hurt her to know I didn't trust her enough to tell her the truth.

Debs was looking at me over mum's shoulder. I said, 'I wanted to go and play by the river instead and Debs had to look after me.' I lied to my mum. **That was my second sin.**

For some reason my mum looked relieved and said it was OK and stroked my hair. She said I only had to go to church until I was old enough to decide for myself.

You'd think my sister would be grateful, but she isn't. She goes red whenever I look at her; she pokes me and tells me to stop staring.

In the confessional box the priest is silent.

'Well, you shouldn't miss Mass now and you shouldn't tell lies to your mother.'

'Even though she's not a Catholic, Father?'

'Even so.'

'I won't then,' I say and wait to hear the rest.

But he only says what he always says: 'Now you'll say a prayer for your mother and your sister won't you? And one for me.'

On top of these I get a penance of five Hail Marys and an Act of Contrition.

Out of the box and back in the church, I kneel and say the prayers, counting each one on my fingers.

I stare at the red flame and wonder if God really is watching me, watching over me, now, as I say my prayers, at night when I'm asleep, and when I get undressed and into the bath.

Or is it just a night-light in a red jar?

For a moment the flame bends low, jumps and seems to disappear; I gasp. Then the sound of a door closing (Father Treavey off for his tea) kills the draught and the perpetual light flares up again. When I leave, it is still burning.

Burying Dad

When the woman comes who is thinking of buying the house, Susannah brings her out through the French windows and into the garden. The blackbird clatters his usual alarm and flies out of the blue hydrangea bush, but neither woman takes much notice.

The woman who is thinking of buying the house asks questions and looks around at the shrubs and the neat lawn, the empty borders. Susannah offers tea and the offer is accepted. Susannah is pleased: they will sit at the wrought iron table here in the garden and look at a wonderful collection of old photographs, pictures of the house as it had been when she was a child.

'I've probably got some poor bird in there,' says Susannah. They are looking at 'Suzie, 1965', a small girl with two sun-bleached plaits holding a shoebox and squinting at the camera. 'In those days they were always flying into the French windows or falling out of nests, or getting caught in the fruit cage.' They had all died, of course, to be respectfully interred in the flowerbeds.

The woman looks beyond the little girl in the photo, to the house. 'Why it looks hardly changed,' she says. (In desperate need of modernisation, she will tell her husband later.)

'Yes, it does look very much now as it used to,' says

Susannah. 'Though I notice little things of course. The plants must be taller than when I was a girl, but when I think back, when I *remember*, the rooms and the garden did seem bigger then. Look. There's my father.'

They regard a black-and-white photo: the head of a man buried up to his neck in sand. His hair has been pushed up into a cockscomb, a hairstyle inflicted by the young Susannah. His just-awake eyes are rather anxious and he wears a chimp's grin, as if alarmed by the weight of warm sand. 'Weymouth1968'. He shouldn't have fallen asleep.

He could have stayed awake if he'd really wanted to. But instead of moving, raising himself on his elbow to look, he had stayed quite still and allowed sleep to lift him up; he drifted like the waves washing and leaving the shore. Nearby there would have been the knocking of plastic spade on bucket. The sift and slice of Susannah's digging was close to his ears; other sounds from other children – cries, wails and splashes – hung and swooped like kites on the breeze. Someone trudged past and grains of sand lodged in his hair.

'Burying Dad on the Beach.' The woman reads the rest of the caption aloud.

'We were lying in a little depression which made it all the easier to dig him in,' says Susannah. 'He fell asleep; I got bored. I could have wandered off or gone for a swim without him, but I knew he'd be worried about me, so I buried him instead.' She had done it very gently. The sand had been powdery and warm. She'd heaped it up against his sides and then between his legs and arms and then on top, little by little so as not to wake him. 'In the end I was able to bury him quite deep,' says Susannah, sounding satisfied.

'No wonder he looks worried,' says the woman.

'He wasn't supposed to fall asleep,' says Susannah quite sharply. Then her voice softens. 'But he *was* exhausted.'

Exhausted, from nursing her mother. They'd left her for the afternoon, with their newly installed telephone by the bed and a neighbour popping in, so that Susannah could have a day out in her summer holidays; a day spent away from the house and garden. Susannah had been promised a swim but her father had fallen asleep. She hadn't even reached the water.

'Say cheese,' Susannah said the instant he awoke. She was already pointing the camera, and clicked just before he pulled himself out of the beach, stood up and let the sand slide off him.

In the silence it seems she is considering whether to take the woman into her confidence. 'It was hard for us to be happy when my mother was at home dying,' she says at last.

The woman sets her cup down awkwardly with a clash of china and spoon. 'I'm so sorry,' says the woman.

Susannah takes no notice; she is gazing at the house. 'She had a bed downstairs, to look out of the French windows. She could have seen us sitting here now.' Susannah gives herself a little shake and turns back to the photo album.

'Is that her?' says the woman. 'She looks very happy then.'

'Oh, no,' says Susannah. 'That's *Julie*.'

'Julie 1972' is standing on a newly pink patio: a big blonde woman with a broad smile, her body half-turned to the camera. Behind her are picture windows and a set of new patio doors half slid-open. Julie wears a flowery pink tunic and white trousers. In her right hand is a raised glass, in her left she's holding a barbecue fork.

'Oh!' says the woman.

'Hmm?' says Susannah.

'Well for a moment I thought it was a different house, but it's here, isn't it?'

'Yes, it is.'

'But where are the French windows?' They had been there at the beginning of the album among the black-and-white photos and they were there now on the other side of the lawn.

'My mother loved those French windows,' says Susannah. 'I don't think patio doors were the thing.' Or a patio for that matter. 'It was up to me to put things right.'

Julie was the sort who was always wanting something new,

she explained: any old rubbish as long as it cost money. That was Julie: always changing things just for the sake of it. As well as getting new furniture and redecorating, Julie had rearranged the shrubs in the garden. She got Susannah's father to dig them up and move them. Then she'd change her mind and want them moved again. He said the bushes flinched whenever he walked past. And all the little bones, the skulls and rib cages of those once-cherished songbirds, had been dug up and scattered on the earth until they bleached and crumbled away.

'Not long before my father died she said she wanted decking and a water feature. But dad, I know, agreed with me: we didn't want that Mississippi-riverboat look here. It would have been quite out of place.'

The woman who has been thinking of buying the house shifts in her chair and steals a look at her watch. It is a lovely house. She has almost decided she wants it. The old-fashioned charm of the furnishings is not to her taste but that doesn't matter; she can change everything.

'I've never been much good at things,' says Susannah. 'I wanted to be: I mean I had ambitions and I did try. I would have been happy if I could have been a singer, but I don't have much of a voice. I didn't do well at school. I wasn't much good at keeping things alive, even. But I loved my mum and dad and I love this house.' Susannah sighs. 'Dad loved it too. But to *her* it was just something to play with. You know, after they sent me away to school I came back for one summer holiday and she'd changed all the things in my room: the curtains, the carpet, the lampshades, the furniture, even the colour of the walls. My old wallpaper with the farmyard animals was gone. She said it was too young. And my old soft toys were in a box in the attic. When I found them, well, I could see they weren't for me any more. But it would have been kinder to let me decide.'

The woman frowns; surely she has just seen such a room upstairs? With the farmyard wallpaper and the delegation of old stuffed toys piled up on the single bed? The woman clears her throat. 'About the asking price…'

'I'm only selling up because of her... she wants her cut, you know. So I suppose I must get as much as I can for the place. I won't come down.' There is a silence into which Susannah slides the sentence: 'Of course, sex isn't what mattered to him later.'

After a long pause the woman says: 'The house has been on the market for a year now?' Then she reaches the last photo. 'Oh! My goodness!' she exclaims.

'I know,' says Susannah. 'That was taken in hospital. I wanted to remember him as he was then, in his last illness. I suppose I forget it could be shocking. He lost a lot of weight. He must have gone through the same thing, seen it happen with my mother, but somehow I didn't know. I must have been here, playing in the garden while *she* was dying. I suppose I got used to her lying in bed with the French windows open. We didn't seem to have much to say to each other.' Susannah closed the photo album.

People can die very slowly. It's not like in the films where the loved ones gather round and a few last words are said before there is a closing of eyes and the loosening of a last sigh. No, sometimes it takes days, or weeks, even. And you get tired, very tired of waiting. There's no conversation. The person is just lying there, labouring to breathe, not eating, not drinking, not moving, not talking, not even hearing – though the nurses did say it was the last thing to go and to be careful what she said.

For days he lay there with his mouth open and his eyes half-shut. His breathing was so loud, it seemed like the only thing that mattered in the room. Then came the slow ending, when the sound of his breathing would stop and she herself took a breath and held it – until he shuddered and sucked in air again and she could go on breathing too.

She had stayed by his bedside night and day until she began to smell of the sickroom. And when he was dead Susannah had leaned over the bed as if she was already peering into the grave. She was dry-eyed and sharp-focused while Julie was blurry with tears.

'How I wish I'd used a video camera, or had a tape recorder with me, instead of just taking that photo,' says Susannah. 'Because it was just as I bent over him that dad whispered, "Bury me in the garden".'

The silence fills until it is as fragile and heavy as a water balloon.

'And did you?' The woman's words spill out.

'It was within my rights,' says Susannah, raising her voice. 'Whatever the neighbours say.' She puts her face close to the woman's and looks her in the eyes. 'Julie was on the side of the undertakers. But if you do it properly, bury them six feet deep, and make sure you're not interfering with the water table, there's no reason why it can't be done. No need even for a coffin; just get an old sheet out of the airing cupboard, a last look at the face to make sure he isn't "only sleeping", then tip him in and pile the earth on top.' She sits back in her chair.

A certain tension in the air suggests the woman is like an arrow, ready to fly.

'But of course,' Susannah went on, 'someone told Julie that without a will, nothing written down, there was only my word to say it was what dad wanted. But I was his daughter after all; I'd known him all my life.'

Susannah stands up and the scrape of the next chair follows instantly. Footsteps shiver on the new path; Susannah stops by the blue hydrangea. She brushes over it with her hands, and the woman, unwilling to enter the house alone, is kept waiting by the French windows.

At last Susannah leads the woman inside. The tea things have been left on the table, but it doesn't look like rain. After the doors have closed, it isn't long before the blackbird comes flying back.

The Dancing King

Brenda is lying in bed reading a romantic novel when the knock comes at her door.

There he stands, tall, handsome and unfamiliar, dressed in a tuxedo. *'Pour vous,'* he says, handing her a rose.

'Do I know you?'

'I thought you wanted me to take you dancing.' His eyebrows flash.

Brenda takes a deep breath, shakes her head, then swings the door shut in his face and grumbles her way back to bed.

He knocks again.

Brenda bites her lip. Bother. Just when she didn't need a man in her life. 'Come in.'

He opens the door, wearing a knowing look.

'Just don't speak to me, that's all,' says Brenda. 'I'm reading.'

Loosening his black tie, he lies down beside her on the bed. Over the top of her book she can see dark trousers extending all the way down to the end of the duvet and a pair of shiny shoes.

Time passes, and the tension grows with each rasp of a page turned. Out of the corner of her eye she sees him looking at her.

He puts a hand on her arm, brings his face close to hers. 'Shall we dance?' he says. Standing up, he offers her his hand. Brenda smiles, in spite of herself. She turns down the corner of the page. With a snap of his fingers he brings the sound of a full-string orchestra looping into the room.

Feeling at a disadvantage dancing in her pyjamas, without a shred of make-up on, Brenda keeps glancing backwards, afraid she will snag her spine on the corner of the wardrobe.

'Would you relax?' he says. 'It's like dancing with an ironing board.'

Just as an experiment, she closes her eyes and lets herself be moved. His hold is firm, his footsteps certain. It's like floating, another state of being. He doesn't push or wrench.

'You're good at this,' she says.

'Only the very best for you, my darling.'

She opens her eyes.

He's wearing a smile of the deepest self-satisfaction. Surprisingly, she finds this quite endearing.

At last she begins to grow sleepy. He sways with her towards and away and towards the bed, with the subtle advance of an incoming tide. She remembers the light going out and the sound of him slipping off his tie.

In the morning he's gone; no need for Brenda to worry about her morning breath or what to say at breakfast. The sheet on his side of the bed is quite smooth and there isn't a dent in the pillow, as if he's never been there. But the rose on the bedside table is drinking from her glass of water.

The next evening she goes to bed early, unfolding the corner of the page she turned down last night.

'Hello there,' he says.

'Woh!' The book flies up in the air. 'What are *you* doing here?'

He shrugs. 'You called me.'

'I did not,' she says, indignantly.

'You must have.' He smiles gently. 'I'm here, aren't I?'

A few nights later, despite her best intentions not to care what he does when he's not with her, she asks him where he lives.

He takes a drag on his cigarette and blows out smoke before answering. 'The shed at the bottom of the garden.'

'There is no shed at the bottom of the garden,' says Brenda.

'Not at the bottom of *your* garden – no,' he says, teasingly.

The next day she looks out of the bedroom window. The shed belonging to the house next door is quite close to her fence. Brenda turns back to make the bed; there is just a slight crease in the sheet where his body has lain and she hesitates before smoothing it away.

'I wonder if you could help me,' Brenda says to her neighbour. 'I've lost my kitten and I think it might have accidentally gotten into your shed.'

'Nah,' says the neighbour. 'Door's been shut for days. I've had the flu.' He waves a snot-frozen hanky.

Brenda stands firm. 'I thought I heard it crying in there. Perhaps it got in some other way?' The neighbour is sceptical but gives Brenda the key so she can have a quick look and set her mind at rest.

Down the garden path she goes, her heart leaping. The shed door is secured by a large, well-oiled padlock. The key slides in and turns easily.

Inside the shed it is dark and smells of old garden tools, clay pots and compost. There's no bed, other than a folded-up canvas sun-lounger, and no clothes or shoes or other things. She does find a blue-and-white striped mug hanging on a hook, with a stain of old coffee inside. The windows are jammed with dirt and cobwebs.

'No sign of the cat,' she tells the neighbour. 'Thanks.'

That night her lover does not appear. She curls up in the bed to have a good cry, then reads herself to sleep. In the morning she finds she's slept on her book and buckled its pages.

'Where've you been?' These are the first words out of her mouth when she bumps into him outside Woolworth's.

He hasn't been round for days. Relaxed but friendly, she'd said to herself, that's what I must be next time I see him, whenever that might be, relaxed *and* friendly. But she hears herself saying, 'Where've you been?' instead; and within two minutes they're having a row and she's shaking.

Later, she feels so sorry for misjudging him. He'd wanted to see her, of course he had. The truth was he'd been on his way over to her place the other night when he'd noticed a woman about to give birth in the doorway of Marks & Spencer. By the time he'd had a chance to call, it was already very late.

'What did she have?' asks Brenda.

'A boy, a ten-pounder. Really quite something. She's calling it after me.'

He even has a creased Polaroid to show her, of a sweaty-haired woman lying back on her pillows with a tired smile, and himself standing up, wearing a wide grin and a green hospital gown, holding a new baby in his arms.

Later, after sex (forgiving, tender, urgent), while they are mid-snuggle, she mumbles to him in a sleepy and contented voice, 'You can always call. I don't mind if it's late. I lie awake anyway, reading.' But just as she falls over the rim of sleep she thinks: isn't it odd that I don't even know his name? And now he's given it to someone else's child.

That summer, they go on holiday together for two weeks, driving and dancing around Scotland. They laugh at each other's jokes. Sometimes they get lost.

'It doesn't matter,' says whoever's at the wheel. 'We're bound to end up somewhere in the end.' They dance during the day among the heather and look out for hotels with ballrooms.

She hears him whistling in the bathroom when she wakes. He gets up early to shave so that his chin will be smooth when he kisses her. While he's doing that she chews gum and applies subtle touches of make-up. When she hears him pull the plug, she wraps the gum in its silver paper and hides it under her book. He finds her smiling sweetly, eyes closed, ready to be woken with a kiss.

Sometimes though, at dinner, they don't have much to say and she glances about, wondering if she would prefer to be talking to someone else; but then she looks sharply at him, wondering if he's thinking the same thing. Given the chance, they take to the floor and glide until she is happy again.

He moves in with her. When the first night comes when neither of them wants to dance, it feels as if something has ended. Brenda reaches for her long-neglected book. But he says, 'I need to go to sleep now. Got an early start.' She puts out the light, but then lies awake, wondering whether to cuddle up to him; for the first time the bed feels too hot with him in it.

To show her adaptability she buys herself a torch for reading in bed when he wants the light out. In the winter she changes this for a lamp on a headband, so she can keep at least one hand at a time under the duvet. He laughs at her. Without speaking or looking up from her book, she brushes her icy fingers along his thigh. He stops laughing and yelps.

Some time later, he's calm enough to try sleeping. He turns on his side and puts his back to her, mumbling, 'And you've got a cold bottom.'

But she's always had a cold bottom; he's supposed to like warming it up.

Around Christmas time he goes out a lot without her; she accuses him of dancing with someone else.

'You're paranoid,' he says, fumbling with his black tie.

'Here, let me.' She nips at his fingers till he lets go of the strip of silk and allows her to knot it for him.

He kisses her on the cheek, saying, 'Don't wait up.'

In the week before Valentine's Day, he disappears. It doesn't look, at first, as if he means to stay away. His razor is left unrinsed in the bathroom; his shirts are on a hanger, waiting to be ironed; his socks are strewn across the bedroom like the droppings of a large and restless herbivore.

When all the socks have turned quite stiff, she puts them in an old pillow-case. But the laundry basket is never empty while they are in it.

A month later, opening the bedroom window, she extracts a corrugated sock and lobs it onto the roof of next door's shed. Soon the pillowcase is empty.

That night, to distract herself from saw-edged emotions which are trying to cut her in half, she browses the half-read pile of books by her bed. Every time she feels like crying she makes herself read another sentence.

One evening, when she can think about signing up for contemporary dance classes without weeping, he knocks on her door.

'I've got my dancing shoes on,' he wheedles through the lock.

Brenda says nothing. At last he goes away.

The next evening she is tensed for his return. Tap, tap, tap. He calls to her through the keyhole, 'Let me in.'

She turns out the light and says nothing, even though she wants to yell at him. Or weep and open the door.

On Saturday he comes round at midnight, drunk.

'Go away!' she shouts.

All is quiet. Brenda wonders if he is preparing to climb the drainpipe and try to get in at the window. She stays sitting up in bed for some time, straining to hear. But there is nothing.

The summer comes and the evenings are so light and so sad. She reads and reads and reads. How glad she is to have the big cool quiet bed to herself. But her feet twitch and, having turned out the light, she often hears music coming from the garden of a house close by, a deep familiar voice, and twirls of carefree laughter.

These sounds are just loud enough to keep her from falling asleep.

Invitation

When she hears she is going to die soon, mother decides to hold a party.

'I'll have it in hospital if need be,' she says, worried about delay. 'Let them come before I start to smell bad.'

She calls it '... an opportunity for some last precious hours of intimacy and pleasure.'

I foresee a lot of awkwardness and a shortage of chairs.

The hospital on a Sunday. Extended visiting hours. In the centre of the main hall is a café with round tables at which people sit on black and steel chairs, under a glass dome; simulated *al fresco*, no umbrellas necessary. People are eddying in and out of an open-fronted shop which sells a little bit of everything: gifts, newspapers, cuddly toys, sandwiches.

In here are people quietly queuing: buying flowers, tissues, sweets and magazines. There is a comforting aroma of coffee; an *espresso* machine clears its throat. From the main hall comes an almost industrial hum of human voices. The shop till chirps as if it lives in a permanent electronic springtime.

I buy some books of first class stamps, cross the flow of people in the hall and go right up to the glass wall on the far side. From here I can look down into an atrium, where tall plants grow, and water runs over black and grey pebbles and around fallen logs. There are no seats and no people in there. No animals or birds that I can see. Probably no sound either.

There is a mild 'splat' behind me and people stop talking. I look round to see a little girl in a blue coat face down on the floor, still holding on to the hand of a good-looking man in a dark blue suit. People are holding their breath, waiting to see if she will cry. She opens her mouth but no sound comes. The man pulls her up quickly by the hand, right up off the floor, and as her feet touch down, she suddenly laughs. Relieved voices rise up again and close over the moment.

I take mother the stamps and a carrier bag full of things: a framed photo of me newly aged ten on the bike she had bought for my birthday; two clean nighties and two sets of underwear; a small new tube of toothpaste.

Mother is sitting up in bed surrounded by a choppy sea of lilac invitations. She hasn't looked better since her operation: her white hair is washed and softly combed around her face, the intravenous drip has gone, though her left wrist and forearm are still wrapped in crêpe bandage; she's wearing her own nightie. The pillowcases and the turned-back sheet are smooth and fresh.

I'd asked her earlier if she wanted to choose her own cards from a catalogue. They say there is a greetings card for every occasion, but not this one. I know; I've looked. You could say there's a gap in the market, but I don't imagine it's very big. If there had been a choice, I thought mother would have gone for something bright, like a frantic bear on a unicycle maybe, holding the strings of some coloured balloons as if they were helping him stay upright. Inside, the card would have read: 'The truth is unBEARable but let's not GRIZZLE about it…'. But mother surprised me by saying she didn't want anything fancy. She'd asked me to go to a printer's and order plain lilac. She'd given me the words she wanted to be set in silver type: *'Please come'* and the address of the hospital.

Staff Nurse Susan has followed me into the room: 'Your mother had a bath today,' she says, beaming at me, as if she's really proud of my mother, or herself, or, somehow, of me. 'While her drip's out, it seemed like a good idea. Actually,' she says, lowering her voice, 'we need to talk about your mother's "party".' She puts the word into inverted commas with her fingers. 'It's not as straightforward as she thinks. Sister says there may be a Health and Safety issue. Besides, we may need this room, and she could probably go back on the ward for a while.'

Mother, who is far from deaf, ignores her. 'I think I've remembered everyone,' she says. 'But if you think of anyone *you'*d like to invite, do say. Would you do the envelopes?' I move to her side and lean over to kiss her. As I put my hand on her shoulder, I am conscious of having to do it lightly. 'Yes, mother,' I say. She smells of her own perfume again: *Ultraviolet*.

She looks at me then properly for the first time since I entered the room; her eyes are anxious. 'Daniel,' she says, gripping my hand.

'It's all right,' I say. *I'm* all right is what I mean.

'Is it?' she asks, looking doubtful. 'I do so want everyone to be here; and for everyone to have a good time.'

'The Staff Nurse seems to think there may be a problem,' I say. The Staff Nurse nods.

My mother shakes her head and hands me a list of names. She lies back on the pillows and pushes out a long breath. She's always had this way of holding herself tense and then letting go with a sigh. 'They just need addressing,' she says, closing her eyes. 'I've signed all the cards, and put the names on the envelopes.'

I look helplessly at the Staff Nurse and shrug. Staff Nurse Susan gives me her smallest smile and says, in another stage whisper, 'See if you can get her to drink something. We need to keep her fluids up.' She leaves us. I cannot help staring at the end of the bed, left vacant.

On that spot the Consultant stood when he explained to me and to my mother that they had opened her abdomen, taken a look, and sewn her up again, having realised that her cancer was, as they had feared all along, inoperable. Behind the Consultant had been the Senior House Officer, the House Officer and a medical student. The Consultant wore a tweedy suit, his tie swept back over his shoulder as if blown by the wind; the SHO's white coat was clean; it still bore creases where it had been folded and he had three different-coloured pens in his top pocket; the lapels of the HO's coat were curling a little. The white coat worn by the student, a straggly blonde with bags under her eyes, was rumpled and soft with use. Her every sagging pocket bulged with paraphernalia: notebooks, a dictionary, pens and spare pens. I could see the outline of a banana. She looked utterly stricken by the news.

My mother had taken a handful of sheet and gripped it tightly. I offered her my hand and she took it but she didn't squeeze. I wanted to tell her she could squeeze as hard as she liked.

There are twenty-two names on the list.

'You won't be able to take calls on your mobile,' I tell mother. She's asked me to add her mobile number to the cards. 'You can't...'

'I know. It's switched off.' Even now, she's too impatient to wait for me to finish speaking.

'You're like a pot on the boil,' my father would have said. 'Your lid's always rattling.'

When I was a child she had seemed unable to contain her energy. 'Full of herself,' my father had called it.

So full of herself she could burst. My friends thought she was great. The only time she slowed down was when she was ill. Then she turned herself down very low, until she was like a gas burner barely alight. But she'd always been able to turn it up again when she got better.

'Are you drinking enough?' I ask her.

'I'm sipping,' she says.

On the bedside cabinet is her beaker, half-full of water, with a stripey straw leaning up in it. The flowers I brought yesterday are still fresh.

'When I can't sit up any more,' my mother says, 'I'd like you to bring me some flowers that droop, so that I can see them from the horizontal. And nothing from the hospital shop. I'd rather have wild flowers: borage or some buttercups. A handful of parsley from the garden if you like. I wouldn't mind a little pot of basil. I could eat that if I was hungry. Or pinch its leaves.'

She'd been worried that as she got older she'd look like her mother. 'I don't want to end up skinny and round-shouldered, with a pot belly.' She'd always been so slim. As her stomach swelled, she ate less. It seemed a natural reaction at the time.

I shuffle the envelopes. Many of the names I don't know. Some of them I remember as men I'd once called Uncle. What would I call them now? Some of the names are new: she can't stop making friends. Always talking to strangers.

'What do you want to speak to *them* for?' my father would say. 'Why?'

'I don't know.' She seemed perplexed by the question. 'How do I know? I haven't found out yet.'

'Is it OK if I take some blood?' asks the medical student. She doesn't wear a name badge.

'You don't need to ask me, dear,' says mother, holding out her arm.

The medical student sits beside the bed and taps mother's arm to find a vein.

With her free hand mother rummages in her bag. She holds out her mobile to me and says, 'I know you hate them, but will you take this and deal with any calls?'

I say, 'Of course I will.'

'Give me those invitations now a minute,' she says. I put them on the bed and she works through them until she finds the one she wants. She holds it out to the medical student. 'Here you are, dear,' she says. 'I hope you'll come to my party.'

'Oh!' says the medical student, looking from her to me. 'Thank you. Cheers. Yeah; I hope I can.'

'Some friend of yours again, no doubt,' dad used to say to mum when the phone rang. 'You and your friends. How come you're so nice to everybody else and not to me? You used to be nice to me.'

I remember mum laughing once and saying she was still nice to him, or would be if he'd only stop complaining.

Another time she said, 'But I see *you* all the time.'

Later: 'Because you keep *talking*.'

And finally: 'I don't *love* you. I *don't* love you. I don't love *you*.'

There are some other names I recognise: old friends of mine. The ones who liked to say, 'Your mum's the best.' Why did she want them there? I hadn't seen them for years.

They didn't know what she was really like. Oh, yes she was fun when she wanted to be, but other times, she'd say, 'Don't talk to me. Sshh. You can't talk to me now. Stop talking; I'm trying to think.' And she'd be beating her head and groaning, literally 'cudgelling her brains' to get out some idea she had in there, to let it be born. She cared more about that than about me. The old familiar resentment curdles in my stomach.

Later she'd come and sit with me on the sofa and stroke my hair and say, 'I do love you; sorry I'm a grump. What do you want for tea?' But I didn't always let her off easy.

By the time she opens her eyes I have been through her address book.

'Why them?' I say, pointing at two envelopes. 'I don't even know where they live.'

'Who?' I'm sure she's only pretending to be unable to see.

'These are people from way back. Friends I had when I was ten.'

'You can find their addresses.'

'No.'

'Why not?'

'I don't know them any more.'

And then she cries. 'I'm so afraid,' she says. I put my arms around her and let her weep. I let her get my good suit wet. 'Danny,' she says. 'Danny.'

Her mantra has always been: 'I want you to be happy; I don't care what you do as long as you're happy.' I thought it meant she couldn't be bothered to notice what I cared about.

But now she says: 'I don't want you to be alone. Promise me you'll look on Friends Reunited.'

I say I will.

Staff Nurse Susan pops her head out of the office as I go past.

'She seems to have perked up quite a bit,' she says. 'Who knows how long it will be?' She eyes the invitations in my hand. 'Only I don't think your mother's quite got the right idea about hospital visiting.'

'She's going to die soon,' I say. 'Surely she can do what she likes.'

Staff Nurse Susan is firm. She wants me to leave the envelopes with her until she's had a chance to talk to Sister again.

'Not necessary,' I say. 'I'll put them in the car.'

But in the car the envelopes slide across the seat. If I drive some will slip to the floor and get dirty. I can see that the sweat of my thumbprint has already puckered the paper of what used to be the top envelope.

Leaving two envelopes behind, I get out of the car and walk slowly back. It is starting to rain and I put the sheaf of lilac under the jacket of my suit to keep the cards dry.

The automatic doors jerk open. Just inside the entrance is the red post-box. Into its mouth I push the invitations. I wait to hear them fall.

Transit of Moira

At ten-past-midnight by the Tokyo clock, Gavin started floating down the service corridor. Most of the passengers were Japanese and would be strapped to their bunks by now; the only people he expected to be awake were a contingent from the West Country of England, playing endless games of gin rummy in the recreation pod. It seemed like a safe time to go clean the glass in the Bubble Observatory.

He was therefore intensely annoyed to catch sight of a pair of beige open-toed sandals of the kind old ladies wear – the ones with the patterns of little holes punched in the leather – floating ahead of him, kicking a little up and down as if their owner thought she was swimming. Further up were light-brown nylons, the flapping edges of a petticoat and an orange-and-yellow flower-print dress – an ensemble Gavin mentally labelled 'hideous'. She wasn't supposed to be in here. This corridor was for crew only. She wasn't even suitably dressed for zero gravity! Gavin didn't say anything as he hauled past her, just turned and glared.

She was a silver-haired old lady with a determined but contented look on her face and all she did was nod and smile at him, which annoyed Gavin even more. When he got to the Bubble Observatory, well ahead of her, he thought about bolting the door behind him, but it was against regulations. Suppose she couldn't manage to get back the way she'd come?

He couldn't really leave her floating there all night, like some over-fed, expiring goldfish.

Gavin rose to the top of the Bubble and began wiping the glass with his specially-impregnated rags; gone were the days when he could dream of space travel scented by leather seats and mood perfume. As usual, the glass was covered in finger marks and, as usual, Gavin wondered why people couldn't just hold on to the handles that were put there for the purpose. How many more times would he have to wipe the breath and snot and sweat of the world's most boring passengers off this glass before he could retire? He could count the days, but unfortunately there were still three-thousand-and-twenty-four to go (Gavin was younger than he looked). By then, as he well knew, if he spent all his time in weightlessness, his wasted body would be useless back on Earth. He'd be condemned to spend the rest of his years in space or on the Moon, breathing canned air. But what did it matter? Wherever he went, he was sure to end up surrounded by scuffed plastic.

Earth; people always said the same things about it: 'It's so beautiful; it's so blue; it looks just like a marble'. When he looked down at it, he always reminded himself that, though it did look peaceful from up here, really it was as busy as hell and full of tortures. You knew that once you stepped off the ferry you'd be put in line, processed, stamped, herded, sent here and there, told where you could stop and where you couldn't. He was glad to be up here, on the out-trip, going lunar.

'I always said I'd see the Moon before I die.' The voice at Gavin's elbow startled him.

She bobbed gently, using, he noted at once, the appropriate handles. This ought to have soothed him, but the fact that she was smiling, evidently quite at peace with herself and the Universe, irritated Gavin so much he broke the company code and retorted: 'It's not all it's cracked up to be, you know.'

'No?' she said. 'It looks good from here.'

They were long past the Neutral Point and accelerating towards the Moon, though you couldn't tell how fast the ship was going. Behind them the Earth had dwindled to a bright blue disk; the lunar sphere hung before them, pockmarked, shadowed and mysteriously empty, apart from the sprinkle of red and white lights on the Sea of Tranquillity. Stubbornly, Gavin persisted. 'Neil Armstrong's footprint,' he said. 'I ask you. How does anybody know for sure that's Neil Armstrong's footprint?'

'Have you seen it?' said the old lady. 'I'm Moira, by the way.'

Gavin didn't give his name and he even put his hand over his name badge, as if he were putting hand on heart. He said, 'I've never seen it and I don't want to. You might as well look at *my* footprint in the dust.'

'You're probably right,' said Moira. 'Or mine. Perhaps I'd like to see mine.'

'The Moon is full of footprints. It's not like you think it's going to be.'

'How do you know what I think?' said Moira, her head on one side as if she really did have a mild interest in his answer.

'You'll see. It's all canned music and souvenirs. You can't just wander about. They make you see things whether you want to or not.'

'Is that so bad?' said Moira.

'It is for some people,' muttered Gavin sulkily. 'Anyway, I got cleaning to do. And,' he added as a clincher, 'I'm not supposed to talk to you passengers.'

Without asking, she took a cloth from his pack and began making circular motions on the glass. 'Look at that,' said Moira. 'My face among the stars.' When she said it, Gavin looked at his own reflection, something he usually avoided doing as much as possible. He was wearing the expression of a man with a bitter taste in his mouth.

Moira didn't speak again for some time. She rubbed at the glass with her borrowed cloth and looked at the lights in the dark. 'Have you ever seen a shooting star?' she said.

Gavin couldn't resist scoffing: 'Not up here,' he said. 'And not down there.' He pointed at the Moon. 'No atmosphere!' In the weak lunar orbit things either disappeared off into space or kept going round and round, eventually falling onto the surface, where they stayed, because no one would go and pick them up.

He remembered his first trip, leaving home, when it had all seemed like a big adventure, as well as something to do until a better job came along. How he'd loved to see those bright streaks of burning rubbish flare and fizzle out as they tried to touch the Earth. But now, he knew it was just another kind of pollution. Soon the rest of the Solar System would be polluted too, and eventually the Galaxy and then the Universe…

A flash of diamond-bright sparks flew past the window, ice crystals catching the light of the sun. 'Oh!' exclaimed Moira. 'How lovely!'

'Urine,' said Gavin. 'It's the voiding hour.'

'Isn't it marvellous,' said Moira, shaking her head, 'how even your own waste products can look wonderful in space?'

Gavin couldn't bear it; he gritted his teeth and rubbed harder, as if he might rub out the stars, while Moira made dreamy circles with her cloth. 'I've always wanted to be an astronaut,' she said.

'It's nothing special,' said Gavin. 'These days everyone's an astronaut.'

Moira was in the Observatory often after that, or bouncing off the walls of the service corridor, poking into spaces no passenger should know about. Though Gavin saw her, he always hid until she'd gone away. So he couldn't tell the Captain anything much about her when she went missing.

They had docked in the orbit of the Moon by then, and the passengers had all disembarked. Moira's absence wasn't noticed until the whole contingent went through immigration and the numbers didn't add up. A search was made of the area, all the restrooms were checked, and every cupboard in the transit shuttle was opened. There was no sign of Moira.

Gavin and the rest of the ferry crew were put on alert and ordered to check every locked and unlocked space on board the ship and every item of inventory for clues. Then Gavin was summoned to the Captain's quarters. 'You were seen talking to her in the Observatory,' he said. 'We have it on visual. What were you talking about?'

'Nothing much,' said Gavin.

'What we're after,' said the Captain, 'is some clue as to her state of mind. We're not trying to apportion blame.'

Not yet, thought Gavin. Blame will surely follow.

'How did she seem to you?' said the Captain.

Gavin tried to remember. She had smiled a lot – and she said she wanted to see the Moon before she died.

'Captain!' A voice in the air interrupted Gavin's thoughts before he uttered them. 'One of our space suits is missing.'

At first no one believed an old lady like that would know how to operate an airlock or even want to try. The space suit was fitted with a standard locator device, but it had been turned off. There was a whisper among the crew that murder had been done, and some of them looked sideways at Gavin. He didn't mind: it would encourage them to leave him alone.

Then the visuals for that area were checked again and the whole crew saw Moira standing in the airlock and waving goodbye. She even blew a kiss as she stepped out backwards into space.

That night, with a full set of new passengers safely on board, the story was officially put to rest. It seemed Moira had no relatives on Earth to inform and so the Captain would be spared the difficulty of writing any letters of regret.

Half-past-one by the Tokyo clock. The ferry left the Moon's orbit and Gavin went back to polishing the Bubble Observatory. It was quiet; just how he liked it. But the smell of the cleaning rags caught the back of his throat. Angrily, he rubbed harder.

Then his heart lurched as a star-shaped object crossed the face of the Moon. He knew at once what it must be: Moira in her white suit, spreading her arms and legs to the Sun.

Pressing his fingers to the glass, Gavin saw himself – a ghastly open-mouthed reflection superimposed on the face of the receding Moon – and it scared him. But what made him truly uneasy was the suspicion that, if he had been able to get up close, he would have seen that Moira was still smiling.

An Intergalactic Amnesiac in Search of an Identity

The voice says, 'Open your eyes.'

My mind tugs at my eyelids but nothing happens. Then a finger touches my eyeball and peels back the lid. Light stabs me in the brain; I see, as if through water, a white shape floating.

The details of the picture organise themselves and the form comes into focus. It has long hair and its teeth are bared. Instinctively I bring my legs up and push off from the bed with my arms; but instead of executing with ease the lazy back somersault that would me take me to the top corner of the room, well above this creature who wants to bite me, I can hardly raise my legs. Out of breath with the effort of trying to move, I lie helpless, as the creature bends over me.

'Don't be afraid,' it says. 'I'm a doctor. My name is Dr Margaret McKinnon.'

Over her shoulder I can see off into space: it is beige, except for a long interruption where heads and torsos float by in both directions.

'What's your name?' says the doctor.

'I'm…' That's as far as I get. I don't know what to say next.

'Don't worry,' she says. 'We'll try to help you remember.'

'Look within yourself,' she says. 'Do you see anything? Anything at all?'

I look, but there is nothing.

'I'd like you to try this,' she says, holding open a black velvet bag. 'I'd like you to put your hand inside and pick out one marble.' She bares her teeth again, to encourage me.

'What I want is for you to get better,' she says. 'The bump on your head is healing nicely, but we need to find out, if we can, where you belong.'

She has asked me a lot of questions about:
my name
my age
where I live (alone or with others)
the name of the current leader of this country
the circumstances in which I received my injury
my ability to remember anything.

All is dark. I slide my hand inside the black velvet bag; my fingers touch a heap of rounded, clinking objects, cold and hard. Closing on one, I pull it out into the light. It is a sphere, almost transparent, with a wing of white inside it.

'It's a marble,' she says. 'Does it remind you of anything?'

Something seems to give inside me; but I shake my head. She lets me hold the bag; I bring it up to my face and breathe in the smell of cloth, and air that has been kept in darkness; the marbles click against each other as the bag shifts. I raise a handful to the surface. Some are clear with curls of colour inside, some have surfaces of hazy blue, or are crusted with yellow or milky-red. They look like gaudy moons.

I lie down and close my eyes. Pictures appear in my head and I use the words I have to tell her what I see.

We're outside the dome. My feet are busy pushing the dust into ridges, and flattening these into plateaux. My mother taps on the service window, but the clerk doesn't come. Her irritation is like a low hum in my mind.

We're joined together by a long white cord, which she has looped over her arm. She keeps tapping on the window with the hard edge of her shopping list, a rectangle of white plastic with a keypad and a small screen, which I could be playing a game on if we were inside and I could take off my gloves.

I push my boots together and when I take them away again a wave of sand has formed between them. Pinching a hold of my mother's padded trouser-leg to steady myself, I stand on one foot and move the other, smoothing out the wave with the sole of my overshoe.

Mother gets nervous about air locks and space suits; she likes to keep us zipped up until we're safely home again. We usually go over on foot, even though mother says it's dangerous because of all the bricks left lying everywhere that you could stumble over. But she doesn't like to drive either. She says she would drive if they built a proper road (they could use some of those bricks) instead of letting traffic run across the depressions in any direction.

I wouldn't mind but she won't let me bounce; we have to get along by shuffling because she's afraid I'll land badly and snag my suit on a brick or trip over a brickbot. They're the only other things moving out here and if you stand between them and the sun they stop. They can go anywhere but mostly they only move far enough to shovel more sand into themselves. Then they just sit and cook a brick; so now there are bricks lying around everywhere, just waiting for someone to pick them up and build something with them.

My mother taps harder. Inside, they must hear the knocking; but it's always like this. I shuffle away from my mother, making ripples in the dust as I go. When I reach the end of the cord mum is still at the window. The people inside look at the dark bubbles of our heads and look away.

I pick up a brick.

She jerks me off my feet and the brick leaves my hand and lands with a ploff. As I rise to the end of my tether I see her unclipped shopping list floating near, as if it will be happy to wait until she's ready to remember its existence. But she tugs so hard I somersault over her head and helmet-butt the list. My mother jumps for it but her fingertips just send it flip-flopping away. As I come slowly down she goes up again. We must look pretty silly to anyone watching from inside.

On the way home I want to jump high, to see if I can look over the horizon, but like I said, mother's afraid I'll tear my suit and the nothingness will get in.

The red moon is rising; out in the depression brickbots are working, unconscious of the approaching shadow. One of them lays a brick right in front of us. Like moon chickens, my dad says.

And suddenly I remember: I have a father. Even when I open my eyes, I can hear his voice, calling me. 'Daniel,' he's saying. 'Daniel; don't throw that!'

'Don't throw what, Daniel?' asks Dr McKinnon. I wish I could remember because she seems so pleased with me. She's all teeth. 'Did he mean the brick?' But that can't be it.

'You haven't been listening!' I tell her.

'Don't worry,' says Dr McKinnon. 'You've done well.'

Apart from Dr McKinnon I have visits from the dietician, the physical therapist, a lady with a trolley full of books and a woman who brings tea. I don't know their names.

Dr McKinnon has her name printed neatly on a badge fixed to the lapel of her white coat. There is a nurse in blue and he has his name written on a strip of paper tape, stuck to his blue tunic. I can read it. 'Marion,' I say, pointing.

He makes the surprised face, looks down at his name, and laughs. 'My bad handwriting,' he says. 'It's really *Marlon*.'

I sit in the big chair beside the bed while he changes the sheets. All the time he is chuckling at my mistake and shaking his head. Then he looks at me sideways as he tucks in a corner, and says, 'You know, Marion's a girl's name.'

'Is it?' I say.

'Sure it is,' says Marlon.

But then it turns out there was once a man called Marion. Dr McKinnon knows about him. He was a film star, she says, and he changed his name to John Wayne.

'John Wayne?' says Marlon, when I tell him. 'The cowboy? No way!'

There are more sessions with the black velvet bag, but now the marbles don't remind me of anything. They're just marbles.

'Sometimes,' I tell Dr McKinnon to cheer us both up, 'just when I'm about to fall asleep, I see pictures.'

'Well,' she says. 'Just close your eyes, let yourself drift, and tell me what you see.'

I close my eyes. 'I see stars. Coming towards me.'

'Just let yourself drift; do you hear anything?'

I'm hardly listening to her; I can hear my own voice saying, 'Are we there yet?'

Planets hurtle past the windows. Stars dash through my brain.

'Dad, are we *there* yet?'

He puts down his checklist and swivels his seat to face me. 'Have we stopped?' he says with raised eyebrows.

'No,' I say.

'Are we still moving?'

I look out of the window. 'You know we are.'

'So, it would be safe to assume we're not there yet, wouldn't it?'

But he gets out the map again. I know that he's shown me before, and that I made him cross by not remembering the details. 'Most of the smudgy fingerprints are galaxies,' he says, 'except that one.'

I laugh, because that smudgy fingerprint is mine, and when I put it there he wasn't cross with me.

'This galaxy with the red cross is home.' Father points but doesn't touch. 'This one with the blue cross is where we are going. This dotted line shows our trajectory. Here's our ship, in miniature, on its way towards the blue cross.'

The path the ship has covered is red. The path ahead is blue. There are lots of blue dots still to come. I loll back in my seat and groan.

'You wanna drive?' says dad.

'Yeah!' I say, leaping up.

He never lets me steer on my own, even though the controls are disengaged in flight. They're for docking and manoeuvring only. I know that. He sits in the driving seat and I sit on his knee. He keeps his arms around me.

'Don't wrench the wheel so hard,' says dad.

'But it's not doing anything,' I say, forgetting to pretend.

'Even so.' His voice sounds tight.

I look round and up at his face.

He's staring out of the window. His eyes look as if they're being slowly boiled.

'Were there any names on the map?' asks Dr McKinnon.

'No,' I say. 'Not any I could see.'

I don't know what to call the people who don't have their names on their chests; I want to wear mine so that people will know who I am. Marlon writes it for me on a strip of paper tape but it won't stay stuck to the downy white hospital gown.

'Don't worry about it, Daniel,' says Marlon. 'Most people don't go around with their names on a badge.'

I've learned to walk since they put Jesus into my room. He doesn't wear his name on his chest.

On the very first day, when I'm re-telling him my two memories, he grunts and asks me, 'What planet are you from?'

I tell him I don't know.

'What's your name?' I ask. 'Why don't you have it written down?'

'Jesus,' he says, snorting and turning his back.

'Hello, Jesus,' I say, turning my back on him too. 'My

name's Daniel.' I look down; my name has fallen off.
When you're out in the hallway you can see that the torsos and heads are carried by legs. They're not floating, after all. Jesus goes out a lot. When he's here he won't look at me. I find him sitting in a different room, in front of a box of moving pictures. Now some of my day is spent sitting here. It is called the TV lounge; that is what is says on the door. No one speaks except the people in the box.

Dr McKinnon tells me I have to think about leaving the hospital. When she speaks she doesn't look at my face, but over my shoulder, as if talking to someone behind me. I turn but no one is there.

Where do they want me to go? A man comes and takes my photograph, and then it is in the papers.

'Don't worry,' says Marlon. 'It's nearly Christmas. Someone will have pity on a lost puppy like you.' He says they always like to clear as many beds as they can before the holidays. I wonder how they will get the beds out of the rooms and what they will do with the rooms afterwards. Where will all these people go?

I look at my photograph; my eyes are closed; my mind's eye is disturbed by flickering dreams.

One morning, when I should be waking up, I find myself standing near an open window and see a yellow curtain, blowing in the sun. I put my hand over my mouth and nose, afraid; someone is letting all the air out.

But then I see the curtain is blowing towards me, as if air is coming in from the outside. This is unusual. My legs move; the window comes closer. A hand (mine?) brushes the curtain aside. Outside is a street: the sun beats down on a boardwalk and, beyond that, hard-baked dirt. One long street of wooden houses stretches away towards the mountains, dwindling into an open space of sand and scrub, white in the heat, all the way to the red horizon. A big man on a horse is riding out of the desert towards me.

I step out onto the boardwalk, just as the big man stops outside the house. 'I like it here,' I say to him, as he's getting down from his horse. 'You have weather.'

'Well, for crying out loud, boy, put some clothes on,' says the big man.

I look down at myself and see that I am naked. The sun feels good on my skin. The breeze tickles the hair on my arms. I shake my head.

He shakes his head too. 'Well, I guess as long as there's no one else around. It's your sunburn.' Then he leads me round to the back of the house.

But where is the back of the house? There's nothing but a beam angled to hold up the one front wall of unpainted wood. Yet here is the window of a few moments ago and the same yellow curtain blowing.

'That's the way it is, boy,' says the big man. 'Better get used to it.'

'Good news,' says Marlon. 'Someone has recognised you.' He has brought me a pile of clothes. I sniff them. They smell of perfume, different from the smell on the hospital gown.

'These are *your* clothes,' says Marlon. 'Don't you recognise them? You go along the corridor and have a shower now and take these with you,' – he piles them into my arms – 'and come back with them on.'

I set off.

'Hey,' says Marlon, calling after me.

I turn.

He comes up and spins me around again, tugging the strings at the back of my garment.

'You forget there's no back to this thing,' he says. 'You're walking around showing your ass to the world.'

'Thanks,' I say.

In the bathroom I work the hot tap and the cold and make the right mix. I look into the mirror. In it I see a man with a growth of dark beard and lank hair shot with grey. There are pouches under the eyes, broken veins on the cheeks, red patches around the nose. I look at him sideways and he, suspicious, does the same.

I take a long time to wash, or rather, I spend a long time playing with the water, losing myself in the sounds of lapping and splashing, the feel of the silky flow of it over my wrists, the spattering drops jumping up at my face when I hit it with a flat hand.

My face is wet and now I think I remember… I am crying, as I push the wall with the yellow-curtained window. The big man leaps out of the way as the wall totters. 'Look out!' he shouts, as the beam falls down, and the wall changes direction. As it falls towards me I put my arms over my head.

Marlon opens the door. 'Come on,' he says. 'She's here.'

I nod and show my teeth and Marlon goes away.

Slowly, I get dressed in the clothes they want me to wear. The trousers, when I hold them up, seem impossibly long, something that would fit my father. And yet they fit me. I button up the shirt, starting from the bottom so I do it right. My fingers are trembling.

Slowly, I walk back down the corridor to my room. Waiting inside is a woman, sitting in my bedside chair, talking to Marlon who's stripping the bed and Jesus who is looking at her with big eyes.

I peer at them through the crack in the door.

'It's hard to know what happened exactly, or why,' the woman is saying, in a gun-metal voice, 'he just went off to work that day, like any other, and next thing, he's here. You know,' she leans forward and taps a finger on the stripped bed, 'they found him wandering in the desert, *naked*, not a stitch on him?'

Marlon touches the metal bed-frame and a blue spark cracks. 'Damn,' says Marlon, snatching his hand away. 'Sorry,' he says, 'that static'll get you every time.' He finds the edge of the clean sheet and shakes the cloth free.

I turn away from the door. At the end of the corridor I see Dr McKinnon with a clipboard under her arm, passing on her way to somewhere else.

I stand in the hallway and try to breathe while people move around me, not looking at me, not telling me that I am in the way. Turning, I begin to walk, not looking back. I keep one hand on the wall as I walk, and push, steadily, against it.

Somewhere there must be a way out; somewhere there must be a way to go.

The Disappearance of Baby Joe

Big Joe has a helicopter, large houses and more than one island. He also has a bad heart; his arteries are glue. Never mind; Big Joe has no intention of dying.

He has his own clinic, staffed with the best doctors, surgeons, nurses and technicians money can buy. It takes care of him and all his 'people' and does important research besides. There is a Reproduction Unit, where the latest advances in genetic modification and cloning are practised, but it has been something of a disappointment: in thirty years it has only delivered one viable living product.

'How is the little guy?' Big Joe asks, maybe once or twice a week. He never forgets entirely, no matter where he is at the time: his office in Manhattan, his yacht in Sydney harbour, or the small country he owns in South America. Usually, his assistant glances at the last page of a leather-bound report and says, 'He's good.'

The little guy is precious, the first and last of his kind. If Big Joe ever worries about him he consoles himself with the thought that Baby Joe is treated like a little Prince. A very short, perpetually incarcerated and ultimately doomed Prince – but then, Baby Joe doesn't know much about that. He only knows what it is like to be fussed over by his attendants, whose job it is to keep him happy and ignorant and free from disease.

He's never even seen his dad.

Baby Joe lives on an artificial island poking out into Amsterdam harbour. His palace is a rubber igloo inside a warehouse aromatic from years of storing cocoa beans. Baby Joe wouldn't know about that either: the air in the igloo is filtered and conditioned; there is just the right amount of illumination from daylight bulbs to keep him healthy; soothing music regulates his moods.

There are no windows and he has never been outside. They tell him it is dangerous and disease-ridden. This is true (they show him newspapers) but no more than it has ever been.

'You're too special to risk losing,' is what his doctor tells him. Baby Joe believes it. After all, he is the centre of the universe: a boy, nearly a man, with many servants and no responsibilities.

Every day Baby Joe has a visit from a doctor, a dietician, an exercise coach, a masseur and a nurse (who makes sure he washes properly). He also regularly sees an igloo-cleaner and a psychoanalyst. They all talk to him as if he really is a slice of minor royalty. None of these people are bigger than four feet tall because that is the height that Baby Joe has been programmed to attain. Big Joe decreed the clone should not be able to look him in the eye. At fifteen, he's full-grown.

Last of all there is Mort, his personal servant, his companion; the nearest thing Baby Joe has to a friend.

Mort crawls inside the igloo with a cup of green tea for Baby Joe and stands up.

Baby Joe is lying on a bank of cushions, wearing his favourite purple plush all-in-one. He has a big torso and little arms and legs. He could lose weight, but so what, if he's happy?

Right now he is frowning. 'Are you getting taller?' says Baby Joe.

'I don't think so,' says Mort.

'But your head's almost touching the roof.'

'Maybe the pressure's gone down. I'll get Piet to take a look.'

'The amazing invisible Piet,' says Baby Joe. Then he puts up his hand for Mort to pull him to his feet.

Baby Joe stands next to Mort. Mort sags a little at the knees.

'I think I'd better get the doctor to take a look at you,' says Baby Joe. 'We don't want you getting too big; it isn't natural.'

It is 3am before Mort is measured.

'Four-feet-two,' says the doctor, yawning. 'Unless I'm very much mistaken, which at *this* time of night would be excusable.' She checks again. 'Nope. Four-feet-two. Have you been taking your pills?'

'Of course,' says Mort. He glances at Joe, who is sleeping like a big peaceful baby.

'So how come you're growing?' says the doctor. She was 'capped' at three-feet-ten-and-a-half inches, to be on the safe side (no sense wasting that expensive education).

Mort shrugs. 'Maybe my body just really *wants* to grow.'

'So you need a double-dose? Is that what you're saying?'

'Err… maybe.'

'Sure thing,' says the doctor. 'And if that doesn't work we can use injections or maybe even a slow-release implant. Don't worry; we'll get this thing under control.'

When the doctor has gone, Baby Joe opens his eyes and says: 'What did she mean about pills?'

'Vitamins,' says Mort.

'No,' says Baby Joe. 'There's something else. Tell me.'

'I can't,' says Mort. 'I'm not supposed to tell.'

'I order you to tell.'

'But this comes from higher up,' says Mort.

'There's no one higher up than me,' says Baby Joe.

'There always something higher up,' says Mort.

'No, no, no!' shouts Baby Joe and he throws himself on his cushions and bites them, and sheds real tears.

'You won't like it,' says Mort.

Baby Joe sits up. 'Tell me anyway.'

Mort folds his arms. 'I don't think I should.'

'I'll give you anything you want.'

Mort looks at Baby Joe's purple plush all-in-one, his big soft cushions. 'Got any chocolate?' says Mort.

'Can chocolate make you grow?' says Mort. He is sitting out on the quayside, where no boats are, with Piet the security officer. Water sloshes beneath the concrete surface where they sit; like most of the city, the island is built on piles. Across the water are the deserted docklands of Amsterdam, the scrapheaps where gangs of children used to clamber. The bridge to the island was blown up long ago.

Piet is on duty, so he's wearing his dark uniform, but when his shifts are over he becomes the island's unofficial gardener, growing vegetables in the little park – a patch of wood, wild lawn and dark earth that has its incongruous existence in the middle of the concrete island.

Piet is breaking a chocolate bar and counting out the squares. 'Two for me. One for you.'

Mort gives him a look.

'What?' says Piet. 'Come on. I'm twice your size. Though now you come to mention it I think you *are* getting taller.'

With a guilty look, Mort shakes his head.

'In which case you'd better *not* have too much,' says Piet. 'Because you know they won't keep you here if you get too big.'

'How's the little guy?' asks Big Joe. 'How's my little barrel of organs?' Just lately, he's been thinking a lot about Baby Joe. It's all that gets him to sleep at night, when his heartbeat turns lumpy. He's thinking of getting closer to his clone-son, in case an emergency operation is needed.

His assistant looks at the last page in the leather-bound report and frowns. He reads it to himself again.

'Actually, it appears he's a little depressed. He's overeating. Got himself a bit of a weight problem.'

'Overweight? Depressed?' shouts Big Joe, leaping out of his chair. 'I gave orders he was supposed to be kept happy.'

'It seems that happiness has involved a few too many doughnuts.'

'Fire that dietician!' screams Big Joe. 'Get him on an exercise regime. Do I have to think of everything myself?'

'If we fire the dietician,' says Mort, 'what's to stop him going to the papers, or telling his story to some human rights organisation?'

'You're right,' says Piet.

'Besides, where will we get another one?'

'We couldn't get a short person right away,' agreed Piet. 'But the dietician doesn't necessarily have to speak to Baby Joe. After all, he's never seen me, but that doesn't stop me doing my job.'

'I think it's best to leave things as they are,' says Mort.

'What do you mean there's been a fire?!' shouts Big Joe.

His assistant reads out the latest report, in full.

Baby Joe had agreed to give up the doughnuts, if he could have one last feast. But the vat of oil in the catering caravan overheated and burst into flames. Baby Joe's life had been in danger and he had to be evacuated from the igloo. Unfortunately there hadn't been time to cover his eyes, so when he saw giants with fire hoses running towards him, he began, not unnaturally, to scream.

'What's happening?' says Big Joe. 'For years it's been quiet and now when I need the little guy to be happy and healthy and look after my organs like he should it's one thing after another.'

His assistant hesitates before reading out the psychoanalyst's report: it seems that Baby Joe is having an existential crisis. His whole perception of reality has been called into doubt.

Big Joe moves to Amsterdam; but he isn't ready to visit the island. 'We've got to find something to distract him,' he says. 'All we have to do is keep him happy for a very short time: surely that should be possible.'

Big Joe calls in the circus.

It takes a while. It's not easy to assemble a circus made up only of the very short: children, dwarves and midgets. Then it takes a while for them all to be screened, checked, and tested for infections.

At last the show is ready to go. The centre of the warehouse is transformed into a circus ring and the little Prince is brought out of his igloo for the occasion. He wears a silk mask over nose and mouth, so that only his eyes convey his determination not to be amused.

Baby Joe mounts his throne; Mort stands behind him and the show begins. A short dark man is the ringmaster, and there are children and midget acrobats turning cartwheels and building pyramids, followed by dwarves with baggy trousers and red noses, throwing custard; a short muscular man in tights walks the high wire.

Beneath his silk mask, Baby Joe does nothing to stifle a yawn.

Then to a fanfare of trumpets comes the bareback rider. She is a dark-haired girl of perhaps fifteen, in pink spangles, aboard a white pony. The pony's hooves rap out a canter on the hard floor as the girl tumbles about on his back, balancing, bending, and turning as if she weighs no more than a doll. Girl and pony are tiny, but perfectly proportioned; and they look as if they are having fun.

Mort can't take his eyes off her. Neither can Baby Joe.

A week later, Big Joe receives some reassuring news: 'Your son has upped his exercise regime,' says the assistant, 'and he's laying off the doughnuts.'

'Good,' says Big Joe. 'But let's get one thing straight: he's not my son.'

A week later the circus troupe is still on the island. The boat they came in is untidy with bored performers, longing to get under way. But Baby Joe won't let them leave.

'This is what it used to sound like,' says Piet, looking blissful as he listens to the slap of ropes in the wind and the complicated lapping of water.

'Hello, you two,' says Priscilla, the bareback rider.

'Hello, young lady,' says Piet. 'How is our little Prince today?'

'I've been teaching him to do handstands,' says Priscilla. 'He's asking for you, Mort.'

Mort crawls into the igloo and stands up. His head is pushing against the rubber ceiling now and he doesn't even try to hide it.

'Priscilla's been telling me the truth,' says Baby Joe. 'She says she's seen giants too. And there are stories about them eating people and...'

'The person you saw was Piet,' says Mort. 'He doesn't eat people. He's here to protect you.'

'From what?' whispers Baby Joe. 'From the other giants?'

'Let's call it Harvest Time,' says Big Joe, when he hears that his old heart and lungs are giving way. His need is greater now than Baby Joe's. No more waiting.

His Chief Physician and Chief Surgeon look at each other. 'As you know,' says the Chief Surgeon, 'it was always our intention to replace non-vital organs first. So it will take some time to complete the sequence of transfers. The heart and lungs will have to come last, of course. But they can usefully be removed together. Skin grafts can be done at the very end, together with the hair transplant.'

'So what comes first?'

'An eye, a kidney and possibly a lobe of the liver,' says the Chief Physician. 'That will do to begin with.'

'All right,' says Big Joe. 'Let's do it. Make it as soon as possible.' He turns to his assistant. 'In the meantime give the little guy anything he wants. Just make him happy.'

The ringmaster complains to Mort. 'How long must we stay here?'

'As long as it takes,' says Mort. 'Why? You're being paid aren't you? And looked after.'

'We want to leave, that's all,' says the ringmaster. 'And we won't go without Priscilla.'

'I think we may have to get Priscilla to leave,' says Mort.

'Are you feeling left out, Mort?' says Piet. 'Is that it? The little Prince doesn't have much time for you these days, does he?'

Mort shrugs. 'She's very pretty,' he says. 'I can understand he'd rather look at her than me.'

'She's keeping him nice and quiet,' says Piet. 'That's all I care about.'

But then Priscilla asks Mort and Piet if Baby Joe can leave the igloo.

'It's about time that boy had some fresh air,' she says. 'I can't believe you've kept him zipped up in there all these years.'

'He's not supposed to go out,' says Piet. 'The risk of infection...'

'Is the same for everybody...' says Priscilla. 'Come on; why shouldn't he live a little?'

But Piet says no.

One day, when he is digging a deep trench in the garden, Piet hears laughter among the trees and then from between them sees the white pony carrying Priscilla, and Baby Joe sitting up behind her.

'Hello, Big Piet!' shouts Baby Joe, waving his hand as Priscilla turns the pony around and gallops away with the little Prince.

'Mort!' shouts Piet, running after them. Baby Joe looks back, laughing at him.

But he stops laughing when Piet's legs crumple, when his body sags to the earth. 'Turn around!' he tells Priscilla.

'What for?' she says.

Baby Joe is frantic: 'I order you.'

She reins in the pony. 'You forget yourself,' she says. 'I'm not your servant.' But then she sees what Baby Joe is looking at: Piet lying prone, his face in the earth. As they reach him, so does Mort.

'Do something,' says Baby Joe.

'Help me,' says Mort. Between the three of them they manage to turn Piet over.

'It's no good,' says Mort, getting up from his knees. 'He's gone.'

'Why did it happen?' says Baby Joe.

'It happens,' says Mort. 'Nobody lives forever.'

'What shall we do with him?' says Priscilla. 'What about his family?'

Mort shakes his head.

The three of them decide to bury Piet's body in the garden. 'Not here though,' says Mort. 'We don't want him feeding the runner beans; let's dig a hole for him under a tree.'

It is Mort who digs between the tree roots. At last his spade knocks something hard. 'Hello,' he says. 'Are we down to the concrete again?' But here the concrete is not whole. The roots have broken through it. 'Look,' says Mort. 'It's the bottom of the island.'

He scrabbles about and there are splashes as lumps of concrete fall into the water. Mort puts his head down between the tree roots. 'Look at that,' he says. There is the water, four or five feet below. Beneath the surface of the island there is another world, of tangled roots. At first these seem impenetrable, but then he sees chunks of daylight, not so far away.

Instead of burying Piet, they slide his body into the water. 'It doesn't seem right somehow,' says Priscilla.

'Believe me,' says Mort. 'He won't mind.'

'When they find out he's gone, they'll send someone new,' says Mort. 'I think it's time for the circus to leave – and you should go with them.'

But Baby Joe is too afraid.

Piet's disappearance has the security guards on edge. They are glad to see the circus leave and will do nothing to stop Priscilla going with them.

When he sees that the giants won't stop her, when he sees Mort escort Priscilla to the gangplank, Baby Joe bursts into tears.

'Stop crying,' says Mort. 'It can't be helped now.'

A week later, Baby Joe wakes up in his usual bed wearing an eye patch. His back is sore.

'What's happened to me?' he asks.

The nurse smiles and says, 'You're fine.'

It's a while before they let him have visitors.

Mort is the first.

'Go away,' says Baby Joe.

'It's all right, Nurse,' says Mort. 'You can leave us.'

Mort squats down next to Baby Joe's bed and looks him in the eye. 'You can trust me,' whispers Mort.

'Shut up,' says Baby Joe.

'Just get better. And be ready to leave when I tell you.'

'Why should I?'

'What do you think will happen if you stay? The giants are going to eat you!'

It is another week before Piet's body is found, entangled in a rope hanging off the back of the island. Everyone goes down to watch him being hauled out of the water. There is much speculation. Surely Piet could swim – so did he throw himself off in a fit of remorse? Now that bits of Baby Joe are missing, no one can pretend they don't know what he's destined for. People are talking of leaving: perhaps someone gave Piet a push?

Nobody thinks that it might just have been his time.

'Now,' says Mort. He makes Baby Joe wear a long overcoat over his purple all-in-one. 'When you can,' says Mort, doing up the buttons on the overcoat, 'ask Priscilla to take you shopping. You need some new clothes.'

In the park, Mort digs between the tree roots, down to the twigs and branches covering the hole. Kneeling, he whistles.

When Baby Joe sees Priscilla's face appear from below wearing a big welcoming grin, he starts to cry again.

'Don't wait,' says Mort. 'Go now.' He helps Baby Joe to climb down.

'But aren't you coming?' says Priscilla.

'No,' says Mort, looking down at them. He smiles. 'I'll see you both later.' He piles the branches and twigs back over the hole. Earth and leaves fall on Baby Joe and Priscilla; they move away under the island, clambering over tree roots in the dark.

'What now?' says Baby Joe.

'Ssh!' says Priscilla. 'The boat is over here. We'll have to wait quietly till night falls; then we can cross the water.'

They sit in the boat for some time without speaking. Baby Joe wonders how long Priscilla has been hiding there waiting to rescue him. She's shivering. He takes off the long overcoat and puts it round her shoulders.

She passes her arms through the sleeves and buries her hands in the pockets. 'What's this?' she says, taking out a small slab wrapped in silver foil.

'Give it to me,' says Baby Joe. He holds the slab to his nose. 'Almost certainly,' he says, inhaling deeply, 'this will be the last of the chocolate.' He breaks it in half. 'Here.'

His one remaining eye is bright. 'Good old Mort.'

When Big Joe's helicopter lands on the island, no guard lines up to salute him.

'Where the hell is everyone?' says Big Joe.

'Like I told you, sir,' says his assistant, 'we've heard nothing from the island for twenty-four hours.'

'Well, I want you to find them, wherever they are,' says Big Joe. 'And then I want them all fired.'

'Yes, sir,' says the assistant. He consults his map. 'The warehouse is this way, sir.' The assistant leads the way.

The doors to the warehouse are wide open. The two men

stop at the entrance, looking at the big rubber igloo. It squats in silence.

'Do you want me to go in first?' says the assistant.

'No,' says Big Joe. 'I've waited long enough. You stay out here and keep watch.'

To enter the igloo Big Joe has to get down on his hands and knees; his assistant looks the other way as Big Joe crawls into the tunnel. It's a tight fit. What if no one's there? Big Joe panics, his breath comes in stutters, and then he wriggles out the other side.

Locking eyes for the first time with the boy on the throne, Big Joe tries to rise to his feet. His heart is a small fist punching the wall of his chest. He opens his mouth but no words come.

'Guess who,' says Mort, raising his hand. 'Don't get up, Joe. I've waited long enough. This is it.'

The Love I Carry

Christmas, and I carried my love to Cardiff. I took it with me round the shops, ready to give it to the right person – if only I should see him. The crush of people was intense, but the love I bore was so large, so evident, people moved out of its way.

The air was cold but freshly so; I liked it. And I was free to look about me and move at my own pace because I didn't have my head trapped between the items on a long Christmas list. Other shoppers had to hurry and frown because their lists were very long indeed and there was still so much to do before people far and near (and sometimes dear) could have their perfect Christmas. My list was very short: two items. I already knew what I wanted.

First I bought the miniature radio. A young assistant saw my love; his eyes shone on me as he took my money and handed me the bag. But I knew he would be frightened, were I to offer him my love right then and there: it would be too generous, too heavy, too much. So I took the radio and my love away with me and carried them along Queen Street and into Boots where I expected to find a present for my father. I had to take my love in with me. I could hardly leave it outside, tethered like a dog; anyone might want it, try to take it home. I wasn't ready for that.

A travelling shaving mirror, my mother had said. I looked

for the mirror; I looked for the man. I found the mirror halfway down the shop; it took me a long time to get there. On the way I glimpsed men who were like him, in parts: a hairstyle, a coat, the height of him, never the right smell though – perhaps I didn't know it well enough, I had no memory of the scent of his neck. He was there, I could feel it, among the people, but all in pieces, while my love was solid and, all the time I carried it, quite heavy.

It hadn't always been like this. My love had been light, without form, diffused throughout my body. It had surged through my heart, riding the red blood cells, surfacing in my lungs like a fish. But I'd managed, by some alchemy of good sense, to compress love into a thing I could carry – this density of wanting. So I held it, ready to give it away. But not to anyone. It was mine and I liked the feel of it in my arms.

I found a mirror. There was only one left. Inside me the dehydrated carcass of my love for my father gave a feeble kick. I've tried many times to expel it, thinking it cannot be healthy to carry this shrivelled thing for so long. Yet I might as well try to rip out my own soul. I wished I could find a present that would nourish the old love and bring it back to health. But my father's not a man who needs anything much except now, perhaps, a shaving mirror.

The cardboard box it came in was unimpressive and a little battered from being opened and closed many times. I opened it too and took the mirror out. One side magnified my face. Around the edges of the frame the glass was marred by smears of glue. Still, it was the only one left in the shop. I thought about searching through the store for a small padded bag it would fit neatly inside. But the aisles were so full of people. Pushing my way through them, to go so far and to have to come back again, would take me beyond my threshold for pain-free shopping. I carried my father's mirror to the nearest till.

Of course there was a queue. But I tapped the small reserve of patience I had brought along for the purpose and remained calm. The woman in front of me was a long time at the check-out and seemed about to explode, for she had just brought a three-for-two deal down the crowded stairs only to find that one of the items was not included in the offer. She would have to pick everything up again – the two wire baskets filled with unwieldy gift-packed items and the three fat bags of things already purchased slumping at her feet – and struggle back upstairs. You could see from her face that she hadn't even liked the things she'd chosen. She'd settled for less than her ideal because she didn't know what it was – yet had to find something to give. On this, the last Saturday before Christmas, she still had names on her list to be accounted for, matched against items – unsuitable ones if necessary.

I paid for the mirror and took my two thin bags and my love out onto the street. At which point, having done all my shopping for Christmas, I was free to go where I pleased. I could have looked for the man in the places he was likely to be but I didn't. My love, sometimes so bold, felt inclined to be shy. Instead I went to a small shop filled with fine foods and people buying them. I bought Welsh honey and slabs of halva, and olives in a jar, things I can't get in my village.

Back on the street I allowed the worries of others to flow around me, while I fastened onto the excitement of lights winking in the dusk. Glitter and candles and velvet to conjure a kind of life in the dark heart of winter. I could already taste the regret I would feel at the end of the day, standing on a station platform among too many people skirted by bags. We would wait in packed rows, unable to sit down, since all the benches would be taken and besides we might lose our chance to board the next train, a train ten minutes late, a half-hour late, a train promised, a train which might never arrive. 'Please stand back behind the blue line!' pleads the announcer. Is he afraid we will throw ourselves onto the tracks?

At last my two presents and my love and I will be carried away from Cardiff. On the train I will sway standing up all the way back to the place where I know, for sure, that the man is not.

At home I will set my love down and there let it rest for a

while. A bit knocked about at the corners but still at the core quite intact; quite as lovely as ever. All ready for the New Year.

Acknowledgements

I'd like to thank some of the people who helped make this collection, my first book, a reality: Jonathan Lloyd and Katherine Lloyd for suggesting that I get out of my van and into a University, in order to make writing pivotal in my otherwise unanchored life; Alan and Melanie for supporting me in making the change and cheering me all the way; Alf and Jo, my friend Siân and my family for being proud of me; the University of Glamorgan and the creative writing staff, including Chris Meredith, Sheenagh Pugh, Professor Meic Stephens, Professor Tony Curtis, and, above all, Rob Middlehurst for accepting me and encouraging me all the way; friends and fellow writers Lynette Craig, Sarah Klenbort and Mona McKinlay for sharing the experience; my friend and former landlady Dr Diana Wallace for giving me that essential room of my own; Penny and John for their friendship and shelter; Bertie the wish-dog for turning up one Christmas and saving me from becoming permanently deskbound; my partner Mike for being home so I could meet him when the wheel fell off my car outside his house one dark night, and for giving me all the love and support I could hope for. Also thanks to everyone at Seren, including Will Atkins, Cary Archard, Mick Felton and in particular fiction editor, Penny Thomas, who has been great. Thanks to Carol Ann Duffy and

Catherine Merriman for giving me an early boost by picking 'Pumping Up Napoleon' and 'The Love I Carry' for publication in *Mslexia* and *New Welsh Review* respectively; many thanks to Emma Darwin and Fay Weldon for their generosity in giving their time and their comments. Finally, for all they've taught me, thanks to these places: West Dorset, Amsterdam, New York, Cardiff, Trefforest, and the Moon.

'Pumping Up Napoleon' was first published in *Mslexia.*
'The Love I Carry' was first published in *New Welsh Review.*
'The Dancing King' was first published in *My Cheating Heart* (Honno, Aberystwyth).
'Scary Tiger' was first published in *Outercast 2: Insanity.*

About the Author

Maria Donovan is a writer, and lecturer in creative writing at the University of Glamorgan. Born in West Dorset, she lived in Holland for ten years where she worked as a bulb packer and then trained as a nurse. She came home (by moped) to concentrate on her writing, gaining an honours degree in English Studies and an MPhil in Writing. She has also worked as a nurse, a gardener and a magician's assistant.

She now lives in West Wales with partner Mike, dog Bertie, and Doris the widowed lovebird, on a smallholding with a view of the sea.